Peace of Chocolate

A NOVEL BY

Mike Mitchell

Peace of Chocolate is a companion novel to the mid-grade reader, *Chocolate4Peace*. Both novels tell the fictional story of the Canul family who carry a special and weighty stewardship. This version of the story is from the perspective of the mother of the family. The Canuls celebrate their heritage, both as Mayans from Meso-America, citizens of the City of Los Angeles, United States, and as purveyors of special chocolates that help people make better decisions. If chocolate and better decisions sound like disparate, but enticing interests, this novel is for you.

The author does not claim any genealogical or cultural connection to Meso-America, the Mayan people, or indigenous people in general. He has served on a Native-American business board of directors, served a mission for his church in Mexico, has lived and worked in Central and South America multiple times over the past half century, and holds a graduate degree focused on Latin America, but he claims no inherent right or expertise on Meso-American cultures. He has traveled and lived in more than 70 countries in the Far East, Europe, North America and Latin America, and has four internationally focused university degrees, and loves humanity in all its differences and similarities. This novel is not an attempt at cultural appropriation, but as a celebration of an amazing people, and their ancient and modern wisdom.

BYBLOS
m e d i a

ISBN13 978-0-9990111-7-1

Published in the United States of America
First Edition
By Mike Mitchell
Design and layout by Kent Bingham
Cover background painting by Julia Dickens
More by this author at *www.story-alchemist.com*

The ego-centric warrior lives a life of glory, mostly battling the fear of obscurity. The servant-leader would rather remain anonymous and ensure the success of the mission and the soldiers that make it happen.

—The Mother of Paco and Adelita

The world bows not to the brutal conqueror, but to the meek mother. This humble warrior faces death while creating life. She is strong because she knows what it's like to be weak. She is mighty not because she bravely wields a sword, but because she pressed on into the dark despite her fear.

—Tio Ignacio referencing the Mother of Paco and Adelita

Chapter One

I LISTEN. THE DOOR CLOSES WITH almost no sound. The silence of the early morning is not disturbed. The secrets guarded by a simple shroud of metal brings a smile to my face and that facial act sharpens my attitude for the day. The movement of the zygomaticus major, the muscle that pulls my mouth sideways and up, seems to be connected to my heart. I feel good.

I am by myself, standing in the basement of a house, my home, that is located in one of the largest gathering places in the world. The people here would never think of this as a gathering place. It's where they live and work and spend endless hours in their cars on gridlocked freeways. Some feel safe, some feel threatened, especially in my neighborhood. Some feel alone, even though there are over 20 million people in the Los Angeles, California area.

"Gathering places," I say to myself. "Palenque. A word with so many meanings. The home of my ancestors in Southern Mexico, and a word derived from old Spanish that means a fortified place, a gathering place. "El Palenque está mudo," I mutter. "No answer from the Council. It's been over a week since we sent in our report."

With that thought I can feel the risorius muscle at the outer tips of my lips take over, resulting in a counterfeit smile or a smirk. It pulls my mouth horizontally but does not affect the skin around my eyes. In my case, I know the dimple on my right cheek disappeared. Activating the risorius muscle also affects my attitude. "Or is it my attitude that affects these facial muscles?" I ask myself. I can feel the difference right away. My meeting later today seems more ominous. The simple walk up the stairs from the laundry room feels a little steeper.

As I leave the basement, usually the location of so much meaning, not meltdown, in my life, I consciously shift my mouth back into a genuine smile. I think of my family, peacefully still asleep. My husband, Horado, my son Paco, and my little girl, Adelita. "Not so little anymore," I admit to myself. "I can't believe she will be twelve in just a few weeks."

"It's going to be a great day, a *majac* day," I whisper with a chuckle. "Facial muscles? Palenque?" I ask out loud. "Where do these thoughts come from?"

"Paco, Adelita," I called from the foot of the stairs in our living room, up to their bedrooms, "time to get up. It's Friday, and last I checked that is a school day. Summer vacation is still months away. Levántate."

I turned and headed to the kitchen to get breakfast ready. I love my kitchen. After the library, my favorite room in the house. It's not big but has plenty of counter space and our table where we gather many times a day. Cozy is the word I think the realtor used to describe it when we first considered this house as our future home. The best part of my kitchen are the aromas of love, trust, safety, and hope that permeate everything inside its walls.

Only minutes later I was jolted from my thoughts as I put oatmeal in the bowls at the table. "Mamá, what does *ation* mean?" Adelita asks.

"Ation?" I asked, assuming I missed part of the question.

"Yeah, you know, the ending of words like imagination," Adelita clarified.

"Oh, well," I begin, thinking quickly, "*ation* is an ending of a word that describes the result of an action or a process, like accumulation means the gathering or collection of something. Imagination, something you are really good at mi hija, is the act of forming ideas or images that aren't obvious or present."

Adelita was quiet, which is her nature, but I knew there was always something churning in her cute little head. Her dark mid-length hair, matched by her dark eyes defy science that says darkness is the absence of light. Adelita's eyes were always full of light. "Why do you ask?"

"I was just thinking that when you put *ation* words together it's like putting sugar on oatmeal," Adelita replied. "Imagination and observation are both important words by themselves but put them together and magic happens."

"I see what you mean," I said, loving to watch her mind work. She was definitely not a little girl anymore. Whatever she learned at school today would probably not equal this breakfast table conversation. "The result of imagination and observation, the dreaming and seeing what's really there, makes a regular day a great adventure doesn't it."

"It's like going on a safari in the jungle when you are stuck in the house because it is raining outside," Adelita said.

"Speaking of a jungle safari," I said, "I'd better run up to Paco's room and see if he is even up yet. It's getting close to time to leave for school."

"Take a deep breath before going into his room," Adelita warned me. "His tennis shoes smell like everything in the jungle crawled into them and died."

"Good point," I said. "Maybe I will have time to get him new shoes this weekend."

Before calling his name, I couldn't resist looking at Paco, still asleep. Adelita was right, his shoes really did smell. His dirty clothes laid on the floor, not even close to his dirty clothes hamper. I couldn't complain, though. I noted his schoolbooks and completed homework neatly stacked on his desk. A book, *Don't Ask Me Where I'm From*, by Jenifer de Leon, lay open on his nightstand. Laying under the book was the Bible. He was finding his way. For a brief moment I wonder what facial muscle registers peace on one's face, or if it's just all the muscles relaxed. He was almost too big for his bed. He passed me up in height last year and was going to pass up his father in a year or so, in both height and muscular frame.

"Paco," I called out, "get up! It's almost time to leave for school. You need to eat something. Move, vamanos!"

"Right, out of sight, it was a short night," he mumbled.

"Okay Octavio Paz, but sleep's not the panacea," I answered. I marveled at his ability to rhyme even in his sleep. There were times when I got tired of his rhyming, but mostly I loved it because I knew he was thinking about his words. He was trying to make sense while making art of language that most people never gave a second thought. I would take rhymes over the typical teenager's single syllable answers any day. The beauty of rhyming is, it takes more than one word to complete them.

I had searched the internet for an explanation and if there was some sickness associated with rhyming. I came across the psychological condition of clanging. I became really worried. This condition refers to a use of speech characterized by association of words based upon sound rather than concepts. The website went on to explain that this may include compulsive rhyming or alliteration without apparent logical connection between words. I took Paco to a psychologist, and he said Paco was normal, but very smart. I realized Paco didn't rhyme at school, just with family, and he always communicated exact thoughts.

"Out of bed, lazy head," I said in final warning. "Ándale pues."

Paco and Adelita made it out the door, once again at the last minute. Paco needed only minutes to get going with his day. Adelita needed hours. She was often the first up every day, but usually the last out the door.

"Now let's see if I can get Horado moving," I say to the kitchen table. Normally I would let him sleep more. He got home last night, about two, I think. And it had been one of those long trips. And dangerous. Our first ever delivery to Tajikistan.

"They are a key to Central Asian stability," Horado had said. "It's the poorest country in the region and historically the pawn of Iran, China, and Russia. New influences from their southern neighbor Afghanistan, from Pakistan and even the United States and the Europeans have their heads spinning with threats and opportunities."

"The whole country could use the chocolate, but who do we deliver to?" I had asked, unsure of this project. "We don't want to support one group over another. There isn't a specific decision event or decision-maker to deliver to. How do we stay completely neutral and still make a difference?"

"I agree," Horado said. "It's a complex mess, but that's what we do best, plant seeds of time and space in the soil of complexity. Offering a little more distance between challenges and decisions. Those few decisions open the door to improved decisions. Like our delivery to North Korea, we should make a delivery to Tajikistan's Dear Leader."

"Unlike North Korea, the young students in Tajikistan are open to change," I add. "No matter the politics, over 55 percent of the population is under 25 years old. It's the youngest country in all of Europe and Central Asia. I say we deliver to the Youth Entrepreneurship Forum. It's a start." I wonder in my mind at the clarifying effect Horado has in my own thinking. No surprise Tio Ignacio had chosen to talk with him, instead of me.

"What does Tio Ignacio say?" I asked with a little too much emotion in my words.

"Travel safe," he said with a smile. "He loves you, you know."

"That's it, no guidance, no groups to focus on?" I asked, avoiding Horado's last statement.

"Nada, no guidance," Horado answered. "I think that means we do our best and whatever we do will make a difference."

"*Ay caray*, Horado, you are such an optimist," I countered. "It could mean he has no idea either and this whole delivery is a bad idea."

"But it isn't dangerous, or he would have said so," Horado countered.

"Right, not dangerous, just like your trip to Portland during the riots," I said. "If I remember correctly, you got seven stiches for being in the wrong place at the worst time."

"And I'm here now and that delivery made some space for clearer decisions. It's what we do Querida."

And that was that. It's what we do. It's what we've done for hundreds of years. The Canul family mission. I love it and sometimes, I hate it. I've long ago gotten over my pity parties, or wanting to just be a normal family, working out their lives like most everyone else. Yet, there are days when the world, even our local neighborhood, seems to conspire against us.

"The decline of civilization is mostly the result of bad seeds planted from within, not from external threats or natural events that are out of ones's control," I can hear my Abuela say. A little old lady from Southern Mexico, weighing maybe ninety pounds. But if you could weigh her wisdom, it would be more than a whole room full of college professors and government leaders. Very little formal education, but a lifetime of knowledge transformed into understanding. "A thousand years ago, our people began to poison themselves and it caused their collapse. We had already begun forgetting. A thousand years before that we developed a water purification system that was far beyond the Romans or the Egyptians. Archeologists will discover it at Tikal and ask, how did they know? We weathered our own blindness, and we survived the Spanish conquest, but our memories did not endure intact. Many Canuls forgot who we are and what our mission is. One day they will remember again. We plant good seeds. That is all. We do not try to fix situations, or use our knowledge to stop invasions, or change oppressive regimes. Those actions are the sacred responsibilities of the people in the arena."

I exercised my zygomaticus major muscle for the second time this morning. It helped me feel better. I am grateful for Horado, safely asleep upstairs in our bed. I am grateful for our two children at school, learning, growing, preparing for what they don't yet know is our family mission. I am grateful we have, so far, been able to protect them from the burdens of that mission. I'm grateful to be a Canul.

I stepped into the bedroom expecting to see Horado still snoring, but he wasn't there. I stopped breathing. Had I been dreaming that he returned late last night? Then the sound of the shower reached my ears. My exhale mingled with the water from the shower, caressing Horado, even though I was standing at the door to the bedroom. I knew he could feel it. I turned and descended the stairs with peace in my heart. "It's a big day," I reminded myself, "and it will be a majac day if I practice what we preach."

"Querida," Horado whispers in my ear, coming up behind me in what felt like only a minute later.

I almost dropped the spatula I was using to stir the migas I was making for our breakfast. "How is it you can sneak up on me like a cat, but eat like a horse?" I asked as I turned to thump him as he backed away with a big grin on his handsome face.

"That is my *alebrije*," he said, easily missing my swat with the spatula. "My fantasy creature is the cat mixed with the horse. And speaking of mixing, frying corn tortillas with eggs and peppers is a celestial combination. I hope I didn't wake you when I got home."

"Come closer," I said with my best sultry voice. "I missed you."

He smiled and approached. I hit him with the spatula. "I meant I missed punching you just a second ago." He laughed, and I kissed him. Then I turned back to the migas.

"I think my favorite times with you are when I get home from a delivery trip," he said.

"Me too," I admitted. "I slept more soundly after you got home last night, than all the nights combined since you left."

"So, what you are saying is, I put you to sleep?" Horado said.

"Something like that," I said as I scooped half the migas on to his plate. "There is never a dull moment with you around, but when I need to sleep, it is deep and peaceful when you are next to me." I served myself and sat down across from him. Our little home was humble, except for the basement and maybe the library, but it was perfect.

"You don't perhaps, uhm, have a need for sleep after breakfast, do you?" Horado asked with a mischievous smile on his face.

"Not today, Casanova," I said, smiling back. I loved his smile. His cheeks raised, making him look royal. His body was muscular, but his face was like a baby, soft and smooth. "Need I remind you that you got home a day later than planned and we have the presentation to give to the council in just a few hours?"

"And we've not heard a word from them since we sent in our report last week," he stated. I could see the wrinkles in his forehead that only appeared when he was struggling for understanding about a topic. In those moments his dark eyes resembled a cenote pit of clear water at night, dark and hiding their true depth.

"You need to talk with Tio Ignacio," I said. "He's not talking to me, so I had to wait for you to get home before I finished the presentation."

"It wasn't me that decided he would speak to me and not you," Horado said. "At least I have this second value beyond being melatonin with legs."

"And arms," I said. "You can do the dishes," I added with my own mischievous grin. "I will be down in the chocolate room when you're done." I gave him a kiss on his creased forehead and left the kitchen. His hair smelled really good and for a brief second, I considered his earlier offer, but I kept walking.

At second thought, I turned right instead of left in the living room and went to the library. The library was my haven. It was the only room on the third floor. It may be the most peaceful and relaxing place on the face of the earth. I had never been there, but I was pretty sure it beat any beach in the South Pacific. The library is also where the portrait of Tio Ignacio hung. I still checked in with him most every day, even though he stopped talking to me years ago.

"Hey Tio," I said from the top of the stairs. "Horado is home, thank goodness. We need your wisdom before we finish our report to the Canul Council later this morning. I don't know how you operate while Horado is on a delivery trip. I never had that experience when I was the chosen person you spoke with. Anyway, thanks for keeping him safe and bringing him home to us."

I stared at his inquisitive but solemn face for a few moments, looked around the library, and then descended the three flights of stairs to the basement.

Two hours later Horado and I were looking at each other again, sitting in our basement conference room. This time there were no smiles nor playful banter.

"That's the decision of the Council," the voice on the other end of the video-conference said. "We can no longer support your production needs from here. We can ship raw resources. Those were not damaged in the hurricane. It's going to take months, if not more than a year to get our production up to speed. With that kind of timeline, we think it makes more sense for you to develop your own chocolate manufacturing needs. It's either that, or you stop deliveries for the next twelve to eighteen months."

"We are glad you are all safe," Horado said. "You know we only relocated to our new home without conferring with you because of the amazing opportunity. The price, the space, and its much closer to our warehouse. All of that is in our report, when you get a chance to read it. Our manufacturing capabilities are pretty minimal still since we only relocated last month."

"We can do it," I chimed in. "It will be a little more inefficient shipping raw supplies rather than completed chocolate, but we'll manage. We will shift our warehouse from chocolate storage to cacao storage. We can't duplicate our manufacturing facilities in the short-term, so we will bring in raw materials from the warehouse in small amounts to this facility. It's ready to go."

"I don't know, Querida," Horado interjected. "Will the movements of materials and product create curiosity with the neighbors? Somebody is going to call the police, thinking we are running a drug lab. How are we going to explain this to the police and then to the county health people? They will shut us down completely. You know I'm more flexible than a flour tortilla but using this facility to meet all our delivery needs runs big risks."

"We are only your advisory council," another member of the council said, as much for some members of the council who claimed more authority than they really had, as for our peace of mind. "You have both been eating the burrito from both ends, to add to your tortilla comment Horado. Maybe a little break will do you good."

"We will take the weekend off to think about it," Horado said. "I'm glad you liked the presentation. I can't take much credit for it, but it's been a very busy year and I think we have made a difference. When we didn't hear from you, we were worried. We are glad you are all safe and healthy."

"Yes, Horado, we know which one of you is organized and on time," a third council member said with a chuckle. "We will look forward to your decision."

With that they signed off. I let out a long breath. "Wow, I guess we should keep better track of the weather in Southern Mexico," I said. "I thought they were upset with us for moving to this new house."

"So, you really think we can produce enough to meet our needs?" Horado asked.

"It takes about 400 cocoa beans to make one pound of chocolate," I said, doing the math in my head. That's between 30 to 40 beans per bar of our best chocolate bar. It would require a little less beans if we pumped all the junk into the bars the candy companies make. That is not an option."

"I deliver about 50 pounds of chocolate a month and we ship out at least 300 pounds a month," Horado said.

"350 pounds equates to around 14 days of work for one person, full time. We can spread that out to 28 days. The bigger challenge will be the logistics," I noted.

"That's my job," Horado said. "I can get the beans to you, if you can make enough into chocolate."

"But you are also traveling to make deliveries," I noted. "You aren't home every day all month. In addition, our panel van can carry about 500 pounds of cargo. We can off-load it in the garage to keep away from curious eyes. You will need to complete the elevator to this room as soon as possible."

"I can have that completed in a week," Horado said. "We already have all the parts."

"We are still not out of the woods," I said, rethinking my earlier optimism. "In order to produce 350 pounds of chocolate, we would need to make 245 trips with the van each month. That's like nearly 9 trips a day, every day. With your travel that number goes through the roof for the days you are here."

"It adds up quickly," Horado said, also seeing the reality of the flow. "We have about a two-month reserve, right? So how about we produce half, about 175 pounds, and spread those two months out to four?"

"Still too many trips to and from for the time you are actually here," I said. "We have to cut back on deliveries. I was overly optimistic with the Council. Sorry. There is no other short-term choice. Even if we could set up a manufacturing facility at the warehouse, I would have to be gone from the children too much. That would quickly come to the notice of government officials, even if we aren't selling any of this. I think we have to do a little of everything—cut back deliveries and plan for less production."

"Is it time to bring the children into the family mission so we can do more?" Horado asked.

"Not until it's their time," I said. "That's their call, not ours. Remember, I had just graduated from college when I felt the pull to find out more. It sure would be helpful, though. With our equipment, by myself I can produce about twenty-five pounds every two days. With help I could easily cut that time in half."

"You know," Horado said. "There is a silver lining to all this."

"What's that, my optimistic husband?" I asked suddenly feeling exhausted.

"The cacao farmers make less than $5 dollars a day, of which only about $1.90 is profit. That's like $1,400 a year. And that has to feed the whole family. Even with Mexico's low cost of living, that is a tragedy. For a family of four that is something less than 50 cents a day per person."

"And?" I asked. "Where is the silver lining it that?"

"We are now the direct buyers," Horado said. "Before we simply purchased the chocolate. The Council made the purchases from the farmers and then produced the chocolate there. I would have to do the math, but I think we could afford to pay double that wage. We will save some doing our own manufacturing. We don't cost anymore doing our own production. It is also less costly to ship the beans. It's more volume, but unlike the completed chocolate, they don't need to be transported in a climate-controlled shipping container."

"I love it!" I said. "I feel better than I have all day."

"Better than when I was flirting with you before breakfast?" Horado asked.

"Better than that," I said. "But I have to admit I have a sudden urge to kiss you for that wage increase insight."

"Actually, I was going to ask for your insight" Horado said with a spark in his eyes. "Why did I have the feeling you were breathing on me when I was showering this morning?"

Chapter Two

"THAT'S IT FOR TODAY," I told myself. "Thirty pounds of chocolate this week so far. Not bad for part time work." I knew I needed to get to the laundry and find a place in this new neighborhood where I could get Paco some new shoes. Both Paco and Adelita attend the same schools as before our move. You would think the local stores would be the same, but not if I wanted to support my neighborhood. I closed the door to the chocolate room and started sorting clothes. "I don't know if it's convenient or an evil reminder that the chocolate room is connected to the laundry room. No matter which room I'm in I can hear the other calling my name, "There's work in here to do.""

As I put Adelita's clothes in the washer a recent memory washed over me. "I think I'm an LSI," Adelita had announced during our move to our new house.

"What's that?" I had asked her as I was sat down another box in the kitchen, not quite in the conversation.

"A Life Scene Investigator," she explained. "You know, like how Paco wants to be a CSI, a Crime Scene Investigator when he grows up."

"Do you know what a CSI does?" I asked, getting more engaged.

"That's a person who figures out what things happened at certain times and places, usually as part of something bad like a crime," she explained.

"Your brother watches too much television," I said. "What are you going to figure out if you become an LSI?"

"I'm already an LSI. Life happens all the time," Adelita explained. "Why wait for a crime to figure out what is happening?"

"I think that is called a sociologist," I explained.

"LSI sounds better," Adelita said.

Honestly, I don't know where all her thoughts come from. Maybe I shouldn't have celebrated her vivid imagination as she was growing up. It is a God given gift she has but bringing attention to it over other talents might have been a mistake. I didn't want her to think pretending was the same as seeing, or that seeing was the end of the process.

"Your observation talent was given to you not only to see," I explained to her later that day. "If you are going to be a Life Scene Investigator, you must also follow through—like when you observe a rule or a law. If you observe that it hurts when your hand gets too close to a fire, you also need to be wise and not put your hand back in a fire. The same goes for things that you see should be done. When you see Abuela needs help carrying the masa flour to the table when she is making tamales, you should carry it for her, without her having to ask you." I was not sure she understood what I was saying, but I have noticed her taking action, sometimes with hilarious results.

Recently she took it upon herself to hide all of my Mamá's jewelry just in case it could have been robbed. It almost gave her Abuela a heart attack, thinking it had actually been robbed. I felt bad, but I put Adelita on a full day time out. A tough punishment for a girl of almost twelve years old, yet she has ways to remind me she is still my little girl. When Abuela found out what had happened, she laughed for an hour. I think partly because her jewelry had not been stolen and partly because of her grand-daughter's audacity. They are like *dos gotas de agua*, two drops of water in the same glass.

"Mamá, do you smell chocolate?" Adelita asked the next morning before school.

I told her, "Yes I can smell chocolate," wondering where she was going with the question.

"You can?! I thought I was going loco. Where do you think it is coming from?" she asked.

Trying to keep a straight face, I stopped folding towels and turned to look at her. "What are you talking about, Adelita?"

"I'm talking about the smell of chocolate in the house. It seems like it's everywhere," she explained.

I didn't want to give her the real answer, "Well you see, we have a chocolate factory in a secret room in the basement and we send it all over the world, and our family has been doing this for centuries and now it's your burden to carry." Instead, I said, "Oh, in that case at this moment I can't smell the chocolate, only the laundry. I thought you were asking me if chocolate had a unique smell." I noticed she was looking at me with an odd expression. "Are you feeling alright mi cariñita?"

"I'm fine Mamá. It is probably just my imagination," she said in disappointment.

I felt so bad hiding the truth from her. I needed to talk to Horado as soon as he got back from his present delivery trip. Thank goodness he was only traveling to Houston, Texas. I changed the subject and said, "Well, since you are here, can you imagine these clothes put away in your bedroom, please?" as I handed her a pile of freshly washed clothes.

I talked to Horado that night on the phone about Adelita's curiosity about the chocolate smell.

"I wouldn't worry too much," Horado said. "Soon the smell will be commonplace, and she won't realize she is even smelling it."

"That might be the case for Paco, but I'm not so sure about Adelita," I said. "She goes to school every day and comes home with a fresh nose. And if she can smell it, I wonder about the neighbors?"

"A fresh nose?" Horado said, chuckling. "That sounds like Adelita is getting plastic surgery or something."

"You know what I mean. At some point we are going to have to tell the children about all this," I said. "They don't have to get involved, but I don't want to be put in a position to not tell the whole truth to Adelita."

"Let's at least wait until sometime after her birthday," Horado said. "I know turning twelve is not some magical gateway but give me some time to think about this. I know, I will ask Tio Ignacio what he thinks."

"We are her parents, Horado," I said. "Tio Ignacio knows a lot, but he is a talking painting."

"I trust him more than the Internet," Horado said. "Ask your mother then. When and how did she share with you the family mission?"

"You know, Horado," I said. "It was when I came home, just after graduating from college. This is a totally different situation."

I talked to my Mamá the next day.

"Don't worry so much," my Mamá said. "When she is ready, she will know, and she will tell you. The seeds are already planted. She is a Canul. The fruits will bloom when the time is right, and when she is ready. I was twelve, you know, when I asked my Mamá about the chocolate that always seemed to be leaving our house."

"It was a little harder to hide it in those days," I said.

"I will give her some guidance as part of my birthday present to her." my Mamá said.

I didn't think any more about it, until one morning when I let Adelita sleep in. "Well sleepyhead is finally moving!" I joked as Adelita stepped into the kitchen later that week after sleeping in. "Are you feeling up for some breakfast?"

"Mamá, why did you let me sleep so late? I have to be out the door by 8:00!" Adelita asked.

"I know that," I said, "but when I stepped into your room you were tossing and turning and your bed was such a mess, I thought maybe you weren't feeling well and I decided to let you sleep."

Adelita then shared with me and Paco a nightmare she had.

"I was swimming in a pool full of chocolate," Adelita explained. "That sounds fun, but I was scared. I could hardly move. I wasn't sinking, but I wasn't getting anywhere either. I was afraid if I stopped trying to swim I would sink."

Chocolate was definitely on her mind. Paco thought the chocolate dream was "too cool, a pool, you rule…drool." I just smiled grateful to this point he wasn't pushing the chocolate button too. I asked Adelita to eat her oatmeal. Inside, I was in turmoil. I trusted that my Mamá knew what she was talking about and sooner rather than later, Adelita would either know the whole story, or she would demand to know. I just wasn't sure I was ready to tell her. It could, no it would, change the course of her life. I smiled, remembering an earlier conversation with her. Interest in being a Life Scene Investigator runs parallel with our family mission, but she was still just a little girl. I could barely stand to let her walk to school by herself. Living in East Los Angeles had its own challenges. I love where we live, but it provides daily reminders that there is a big, complicated, and sometimes tough world out there.

"Horado, it's time to talk to Paco and Adelita about what we do," I mentioned at lunch later that day. "Everybody is saying wait, but I think it's time."

"Everybody?" Horado asked.

"Well, everybody that already knows," I said. "You and my Mamá."

"They may be ready to hear, but are they ready to handle what will come with knowing?" Horado asked, voicing my typical concerns.

"Have you talked with Tio Ignacio?" I asked.

"I thought you said he was just a painting," Horado said. "So, I haven't asked him."

"Well, ask him now," I said. "I'm the Mamá here and I think we need to stop hiding our lives from our children. I think Tio Ignacio will agree."

"Then it will be two against two?" Horado asked with a smile.

"The Mamá gets two votes, one for each child," I clarified. "It would then be three to two. I win."

"Well, let's go up and talk to Tio Ignacio," Horado said, wisely not contradicting my motherly wisdom.

I loved ascending the stairs to the library. It was the only room on the third floor of our house. I instinctively reached my hand out and touched the Marie de Sevigne quote I had Horado paint on the lintel at the top of the stairs when we first moved in. The words say, "When I step into this library, I cannot understand why I ever step out of it." It expressed my sentiments exactly.

It seemed fitting we locate Tio Ignacio here, with our books and lofty thoughts. All our big family decisions were discussed up here. I could sit here and read for hours. Our ancestors typically built temples with 91 steps on four sides and one final step to the top together equaling the 365 days of the Mayan calendar. Of course, I couldn't create that kind of symbology with the steps to our library, but I did feel what I imagined my ancestors felt when they ascended their stairs looking for wisdom. This wasn't a religious place, but I was sold on this house for the library even more than the space in the basement we have converted into a chocolate manufacturing facility.

"Buenas tardes, Tio Ignacio," Horado said to the painting of Tio Ignacio.

"Buenas tardes Tio," I added. We had inherited this painting from my Mamá when we got married. Tio Ignacio was a distant relative and as a little girl I had talked to this painting. He, the painting, turned out to be a good listener. I shared my plans and fears, my successes, and questions with him. Imagine my shock when, after returning from college with an organic chemistry degree, he talked back to me. I thought I was going crazy. Hearing voices that aren't there.

The voice told me to talk to my Mamá. It took a few days to get up the nerve to ask about the painting. "Mamá, what is the history of the Tio Ignacio painting?"

"It has been in our family for generations," my Mamá said. She looked at me and smiled. "He has stopped talking to me. Is it you he is communicating with?"

"Am I crazy?" I asked. "Is our family crazy? I mean, this is stranger than an Isabel Allende novel."

"*A veces la verdad es más extraña que la ficción*, sometimes the truth is stranger than fiction," my Mamá stated, shrugging her shoulders. "Tio Ignacio is part of our heritage. He helps with our chocolate deliveries, explaining the who, when, where, and how of many of our deliveries. He will also teach you about our culture, sing to you, and guide you in your service to others."

"How does it work?" I asked, still trying to come to grips with this family secret.

"Oh cariña, I do not know the answers to those kinds of questions," Mamá said gently. "We assure ourselves with answers to questions that perhaps do not have answers, at least not answers we expect. The sun comes up every morning. Science tells us how that happens, but science cannot describe the majesty of that sunrise or what it looks like reflecting on the dew of the Chipilín flower."

"The square root of the ash tree," I mumbled to myself.

"What is that?" Mamá asked.

"Something from college," I said. "Miguel de Unamuno, a Spanish philosopher tried to tackle this problem. He concluded that science, in order to understand anything must dissect it. That brutal act kills the living thing. Science cannot fully understand how a frog works by cutting it into pieces. Unamuno's nonsense question was, how can you know the square root of an ash tree?'"

"I am glad someone has attempted to protect the unexplainable," Mamá said. "I have been content with the companionship of Tio Ignacio. Now he is your companion."

"He can still be your companion, Mamá," I said. "I can share."

"You may want to, but Tio Ignacio only speaks to one person at a time," Mamá explained. "There may be rare exceptions to that rule, but I have never experienced it."

Tio Ignacio began sharing with me needs of others and that we should send them chocolate. I was incredibly happy to work with him. It was powerful. We made a difference in the world. And thus it was, until Horado and I were married. Horado is part Mayan and part Toltec. He embraced the Canul family duty with great passion. Following an ancient Mayan practice where the new husband usually moved in with the wife's family for six years and was often known by that last name, Horado took the Canul name when we were married.

The shock came shortly thereafter when Tio Ignacio stopped talking to me and started talking to Horado. Tio Ignacio explained that it just happened. He did not choose with whom he spoke. I had some bitter feelings to overcome. It was hard, but the important thing was, we still had communication with Tio Ignacio.

"Tio Ignacio says it is time," Horado said, bringing me back to the present.

"Ha, I told you that was the right thing to do," I said.

"Tio also says, Adelita will know this herself and will take to this work *como pez en el agua*, like a fish in the water," Horado added. "Be patient. She must open the door by herself."

"Open the door?" I repeated, not trying to hide my frustration. "We have to wait for her to ask us directly? How will she even know what to ask?"

"Patience," Tio says," Horado repeated. "I promise if she doesn't approach us by her birthday, we will sit down and talk with her."

"I think I am going to help patience hurry up," I told myself. Since our children were old enough to eat chocolate, I have used it to sooth injuries, both physical, like when Paco fell off his bike when we removed his training wheels, and emotional, like when Adelita got lost on the first day she walked home from school without me.

That night after dinner, I brought the chocolate out. I guess I was hoping that the presence of chocolate would stimulate some questions. It didn't, just quiet, contented chewing.

The next day I planned to raise the issue to a new level. First, I had some chocolate deliveries to mail and decided to get Paco those new shoes. I left a note for Adelita who would probably get home before Paco and me.

Went shopping with Paco for new tennis shoes and to drop off some packages at the post office, Mamá.

 *Itza majac day!*

I always signed my notes this way. Today my traditional sign off had more meaning as I thought again about when and how to tell Adelita about our family mission. I had started signing notes this way as soon as Paco and then Adelita could read. It was a hint to them, but even more important, it was a reminder to me. The swirl I had learned to draw as a little child at my Abuela's kind insistence. I hadn't learned its significance until much later. I looked forward to the day I could explain its meaning to my own children. Was that part of my desire to share our family history with Paco and Adelita? Would the great richness and meaning it brings into my life have the same significance to them? It might push them away. They may not even believe it. Or would it bring us even closer? Of course, that was part of my motivation to share it with them. My little babies were growing up, fast. Would our family mission become a chain around their necks, or wings? Could I have both? Keeping them close, but giving them their freedom to fly away?

Itza majac day was more than a silly, misspelled phrase. My children have seen this phrase all their lives and have never questioned it. I have never brought it up with them either. They probably just think it's a silly and unexplainable thing their otherwise 'stickler for correct grammar and spelling' Mamá does to close her notes to them. A mix of languages and a secret code that reminded me daily of my duty to my children, it was far from just being a silly phrase. Maybe I was the only one who found its use meaningful. Horado knew I used it and chuckled the first time he saw it in a note to little Paco, but he never said a word about it to me. I could see the reason for concern Mamá and Horado had in introducing our family history and duties to Paco and Adelita too soon. It might chase them away. Maybe I was unfairly reflecting my fear on them. Yet, with this phrase I had been trying to introduce them to their heritage since they were little. And they hadn't seemed to care.

I found new tennis shoes for Paco and took the old ones down to the laundry room to see if a few washings would clean them up enough that I could donate them. They were still good shoes. It's just Paco growing so fast that really necessitated new ones. I was sure I could wash the smell away. While I was down there, I grabbed a couple bars of our best chocolate, the criollo chocolate I called Chocolate Madre, Mother Chocolate.

When the children got home from school, I treated them to the chocolate, and asked how their day went. Like some moms had fresh baked cookies, or some store-bought treat, I often gave them chocolate. Not the candy bar kind of chocolate, but our chocolate; healthy, from our secret recipe that stimulated pause and thought.

Without getting into the family heritage of chocolate, I reminded them, as I had many times in the past, "The secret was and is: most problems work themselves out." "The chocolate gives our patience a boost and gives us something we want to do so we become better listeners, and more patient thinkers." I let them enjoy the chocolate before I asked, "So, any problems or challenges I can help you with?"

"Are we the only family in the world that solves our problems with candy?" Adelita asked. "For some reason I have had chocolate on my mind, like my chocolate swimming dream I shared with you the other day. I am pretty sure there is no other mom who almost forces chocolate on their children."

"Do you feel like I force chocolate on you?" I asked, starting to get concerned.

"Force is a word too coarse," Paco said. "There's no remorse and it's use I endorse."

"No, I agree with Paco," Adelita added. "I have noticed that chocolate is more a part of our lives than anyone else I know. No complaints."

"You are very observant Adelita," I said with a smile. I was getting excited that she might push this topic to a place where I would have to say more, even though I had mixed feelings about telling them. "Did you know that both the Russians and the Americans have included chocolate on every space mission? And chocolate is actually quite healthy. Candy is usually not all that good for you because of all the sugar and other things to enhance and preserve flavor. This is healthy chocolate without all those ingredients." I expected one of them to ask the next obvious question: "So where did you get this chocolate?" But they didn't ask.

Paco in particular was quiet. His thoughts were somewhere else. As if he read my mind, he smiled at me and said, "It was a good day at school. Preparation is my ground rule. I almost got in a fight, but just sat tight. No one got hurt, the attack I was able to avert. Thanks for the dessert." He gave me a rare hug and went to do his homework. Somewhere in the midst of his hug, I realized how big he was getting and I almost felt like to child in his embrace.

I wanted to ask more, but I knew he told me all he was going to say, and I was grateful he even shared these tiny morsels. I would be grateful for that. I smiled at Adelita, who just shrugged her shoulders, telling me she knew as little as I did about what goes on in a teenage boy's head.

Chapter Three

MAKING TAMALES WITH MAMÁ IS one of my favorite activities. I'm now a mom myself and neither Paco nor Adelita show much interest in making tamales with me. Paco always has great interest in consuming them, however. Adelita adores the time she spends with her abuela and if that were to involve making tamales, she would happily help. Mamá doesn't have quite the energy she did when I was Adelita's age. Her body, between those hands and her face, is healthy and relatively young looking. Her hands are wrinkled and show signs of arthritis. Her face also shows her age. Long hours working in the sun when she was young in Mexico might have something to do with that. Her dark eyes now contrast with her mostly silver hair. Her nearly constant smile might exacerbate her wrinkles but accentuates her natural beauty.

The smell of the freshly mixed masa mixes with the words of our conversation. When I was young, I became convinced our tamales had a slightly different taste depending on the conversations during their making. I'm a trained chemist so my mind rejects this idea. But my heart and my pallet are patient with the limitations of my mind. They know the truth. Today's tamales will have a deep flavor, perhaps underscoring the hopes of the farmer who planted and nurtured the maíz that became the masa flour. Along with the lard, chicken stock, salt, baking powder, and cumin, our words are mixed into the dough. I don't suppose the words would successfully integrate with the other ingredients if we used modern utensils instead of our hands.

Today we are filling our tamales with sweet-seasoned chicken breast. We will wrap these tamales in corn husks and steam them. Just like our words and topics change between tamale days, so other ingredients vary. I like to use avocado oil instead of lard, but Mamá insists on lard. Fillings vary and so do the outer coverings. My tamales are always wrapped in love and expectation. When I use coconut milk instead of stock, I change the wrap to banana leaves. I will send some home with Mamá, but the majority we will consume in the next three or four days. The tenderness and strength of Mamá's hands, along with our words and love will nourish our family.

As I completed the folding process and began to wrap the next dozen tamales in husks, I ask Mamá, "Do you ever wonder what you would have done with your life, had you not chosen to take up the family mission?"

"Are you having doubts about your own choices, or mine?" Mamá answered with her own question.

"No doubts about my choices," I admitted, "but I chose after college. You chose when you were a girl, Adelita's age. Did you know enough to make that kind of life choice? Did your parents make it for you, and you just accepted it like a good girl in your era was expected to do?"

"Only after I chose, did I come to understand the history, the expectation, or maybe better said, the hope, that I would keep our heritage alive," Mamá said. "You make a good point, though. In my day there were not many choices for a young lady. Get married and raise a family, become a community support, like a teacher or healer, or become a nun in the Catholic Church.

3 1

There were those few rebels who made other choices by force of their own will, but I was not a rebel and would not have considered or found meaning in those radical choices. Perhaps you would have, however."

"It seems like a miracle," I said as much to myself as to Mamá, "that our family has kept this mission going for six centuries. How many generations is that? More than twenty. The financial means we have been blessed with to keep this mission going has actually grown rather than being depleted long ago. No one has chosen to take the money and run or used it so unwisely that even with good intentions it was lost. And how is it that every generation has believed in the idea that we can make a difference giving out chocolate to help people make better decisions?"

"Many questions mi hija," Mamá said with a smile as she removed the first set of tamales from the steamer. "Only one simple answer. "We didn't choose this mission, it chose us. And God in heaven is the only one who can answer the question, "Why us?" And why just a select part of us. There are many, many Canuls who come from those original ancestors. Oh yes, many questions, but only one simple answer."

"Supernatural, mystical, magic. I don't have clear thoughts on all of this, but I don't believe in magic," I admitted. "I know that Tio Ignacio really does talk to us. He knows things that he could not possibly have known when he was walking the earth. He can communicate to us across long distances. And he can make fairly good guesses about the future. We have millions of dollars to accomplish our mission and that just seemed to fall in our lap. People are still looking for the treasure we have held all these centuries, yet it remains our secret. But to put all that in a category called magic cheapens these wondrous things."

"Perhaps your definition of magic is the problem," Mamá suggested.

"Well, it's not illusion, seemingly unrelated events, or a fiction designed to impress someone or an audience" I said. "It's not witchcraft, wizardry or the practices of some dark occult."

"I agree it is none of those things," Mamá said. "What do you think it is then?"

"It's unexplainable, so who am I to give it a definition?" I answered with my own question. I put the next batch of tamales in the steamer.

"Just because its unexplainable to you and me," Mamá said, "doesn't mean it can't be defined or given meaning. I am not saying we have to decide the world is flat because from our vantage point standing here it appears so. On the other hand, we shouldn't be too quick to discard an event as nothing because we are afraid to label it sacred or supernatural."

"Our ancestors worshipped gods that represented important things in their lives," I said. "The harvest, the earth, sun, moon and stars, water, life, war and death. But those gods weren't real, just convenient ideas that helped them feel better about the chaos and mysteries that are a part of living."

"You always were one that needed answers to the hard questions," Mamá said. "Don't be too quick to disregard all the ancient beliefs. Our ancestors certainly didn't get everything right, but they knew there were some forces beyond their own understanding and capabilities. They were closer to nature than we are today. They observed what we conveniently miss, purposefully overlook, or discount. In some ways we are the pagans. We have just turned over our faith to science and convenient idols like evolution, domination, and many of the *isms* that I can't list, but can recognize as sad substitutes for reality."

"Isms?" I asked. Now I knew where Adelita got her interest in suffixes. "You mean like communism?"

"No, not that so much," Mamá said deep in thought. "What do you call it when reason alone is the source of knowledge?"

"Oh, rationalism, I believe," I said, not totally sure, and then laughing at the irony of my statement.

"And what is the name for knowledge that can only come through the five senses?" she asked.

"I think that is empiricism," I said. "I suppose naturalism is a part of that too. I am not a philosophy expert. I was trained as a chemist, remember."

"Well, it is all a form of cynicism," Mamá said. "Doubt and a lack of meaning can drive a person crazy, so theories that substitute for reality some can't or won't accept, fill the void."

"Some would say your religion is your crutch," I said.

"I would only ask, what evidence does the world have that there isn't a God?" Mamá asked. "I mean, if a person says we should only believe our senses, for example, then what have those senses provided to prove there is no God? They can't say they know, only that they don't yet know. Anyways hija, all I am trying to say is, the world makes these things complicated and then points to that complexity as proof it cannot be understood."

"I love the simplicity and order of your world Mamá," I said, "and I love the smell of these tamales. It brings me a peace that you are settled on the matter. But that peace doesn't last long when I face my own decisions. Some moments I want to tell Adelita about our family history and our mission, and other moments I fear it is too much and she is not ready for the burdens it places on her."

"My simple view of the world doesn't directly answer all our questions, and it's not as temporary or wispy as the steam from a tamale," Mamá said. "Whatever one's religion, be it faith in a God, belief in only science, or deciding there are no answers, our mind, our ego, they suggest sources of wisdom we can turn to for meaning and how to make best decisions. A person who rejects God and leans solely on science, in one instance might be able to make a better decision than a person who believes in God but doesn't turn to him. That is our family mission, hija. That place between stimulus and response, the balance between judgment and justification—that is, doing the right thing for the right reasons, is where we provide neutral support. So, go practice what you provide. Service the decisions you must make with time for the journey from your mind to your heart and back, and if you need a little help doing that, put a piece of chocolate in your mouth. In the meantime, let's each try one of these tamales, just to make sure they are good enough to share with our family."

"How did you get so wise?" I asked Mamá as I put two tamales on plates for us. My mouth was watering.

"Wisdom is the application of understanding, hija," Mamá said. "It takes will to do, but understanding is where the power is. Understanding is more than collecting data and knowledge. It is experience that helps us discover principles. Knowledge of principles and following them rather than our own desires, that is being wise, and in my case, it came with age. It doesn't have to. We can be wise without being old if we learn to align our desires and values with unmoving always reliable principles. That alignment usually takes a little more time to travel a shorter distance."

"I'm sorry I asked," I said smiling at the woman who raised me and almost always answered questions with a statement that demanded more questions. "I know you said that, so I had to ask what you are talking about."

"No, I didn't," she said, trying to sound defensive but her constrained smile gave her away. She put a bite of tamale in her mouth before continuing. "It's just that I have thought a lot about this, since this is basically what our family does, right? We operate in that sacred space where decisions are made. In that space, we can help the decision maker slow down time so that journey from head to heart and back opens the greater possibility of considering applicable principles. They have the time to filter their habits, traditions, expectations, emotion, ego, and raw data. The more that principles guide their decisions, the shorter the distance becomes between stimulus and their response."

"These tamales are wonderful," I said. "I do believe in God, Mamá. You know that. Sometimes I wonder if he is involved in the details of our lives."

"I don't think he inserts himself uninvited into our lives as a regular practice," Mamá said as she eyed another tamale, but not taking one. "We aren't puppets. Where would the meaning be in that? But hija, if it is important to you, it is important to him. If you ask for help, you will get it, in a way and time that is best for you."

"And our family mission?" I asked. "Is this God's doing?"

"Every person, every family has a purpose," Mamá said. "We are blessed to know our mission with unique clarity and support. Whether that was God's direct doing, or He has His hand in our work I don't know. Just like a fútbol game, I don't think God is really interested in which team wins, but more in how the game is played. I can't answer how the Canul family became the stewards of 'better decisions' along with the supernatural guidance of a talking painting, and significant financial support. I do believe God cares how we execute our mission. You and Horado are doing a fantastic job. I'm sure God knows that too."

"Gracias, Mamá," Horado said as he walked into the kitchen.

"Your home early," I said giving him a kiss on the cheek.

"I knew today was tamale making day and I thought I would come home for lunch," Horado said grabbing a plate from the counter. "This kitchen smells like my abuelo's milpa. He used to roast corn at the little hut on the edge of his cornfield when I would stop by. To this day, roasted corn, fresh, warm corn tortillas, and steamed tamales are my favorite smells."

"You are just trying to get out of buying me perfume, while trying to keep me in the kitchen," I said, poking his ribs. "Your machismo won't work on me."

"Ah, but my magnetism will," Horado said as he pulled me close and gave me a kiss on the lips.

"Se metió a todos en el bolsillo," Mamá said, clapping her hands. "You have us all in the palm of your hands, Horado."

"I'll give you the palm of my hand," I said to Horado as I tried to wiggle out of his grasp. "You come into my kitchen, you expect to eat the food that Mamá and I have toiled to make all morning, and then you steel a kiss, all without asking."

"Ay, querida, may I?" Horado asked still holding me tight.

"Estas en tu propia salsa, Horado," I said trying to hold in my smile. He was in his element. A sweet talker with a personality and staggering cuteness to go with it. "Yes, you may kiss me," I told him. "But no tamales until dinner."

He kissed me with such passion I couldn't breathe. I forgot my Mamá was sitting right in front of us. She cleared her throat to remind us. I was so embarrassed I got Horado a plate with three tamales on it before I knew what I was doing, for the second time in less than a minute.

I watched Horado pass one of the tamales over to Mamá. He gave her a kiss on the cheek and didn't seem the least embarrassed. "We got our first shipment of cacao pods today," Horado said like nothing had happened.

All kidding aside, it did bother me slightly that he could have such an effect on me. I was grateful for him and the spark between us that never seemed to diminish, but I did not want to feel out of control or under his control. I needed some assurance of my own efficacy. Sometimes my stable world shifted under my feet, and I feared that was because the foundation was weak. I treasured my name as defined by my roles as mother, daughter, wife, and purveyor of chocolate space. I felt great comfort in my name as a location in humanity. I am a Canul. I have my aspirational and earned names that come from my heritage and tradition. But my sense of self had fissures I didn't know how to face. What was my identity? What was my name that everything else was built upon? I shook my head. Too deep of a thought for today.

"That was fast," I said, pushing those thoughts aside and not sure if I was commenting on the cacao shipment or how he got the tamales and a kiss on his schedule.

"The Council must have sent it before we even had our meeting," Horado said. "It may have been that they had nowhere to accept the shipment due to the hurricane damage and forwarded it to us via the Panama Canal. I will give the Council Chair a call and find out when it was shipped, so we can start planning for the next load. The shelf life of raw cacao is only about six months. I don't want to be swimming in pods and have them go rotten."

"I was thinking about that," I said. "What would you think about doing the fermentation, drying and roasting at the warehouse? Two weeks for fermentation, another ten days for drying, and week for roasting would take about a month. Shipping that partially finished product here to the Chocolate Room would be easier and take up a lot less space for transport and storage here while we processed it."

"You are brilliant," Horado said. "That would simplify everything. And I don't need to be in the warehouse every day for the fermentation and drying processes. I could still accomplish a good amount of travel for deliveries."

"And that would also take away some of the stronger smells that seems to be bothering Adelita," I added.

"The fresh air and larger space would be better for the drying process," Mamá said.

"This is all going to work out," Horado said. "Thanks mostly to you Querida. I know you could be doing a lot of things in your life, but our family and the family mission has and will continue to change lives and make this world a better place. That sounds cheesy, maybe even placating at the moment, but it's the truth. The most important work, said in casual conversation, usually comes across as idealistic and corny. We both know its anything but that."

"Said to sooth me or not, thank you for those words," I said. "I am not worried about our part in this important mission. I am anxious about bringing two innocent children into the demands of this rough and crude world. Mamá and I have been talking about it all morning."

"Then you are in the best of hands," Horado said. "And that is not meant to sound placating either," he added looking at Mamá. "I have my strengths. Some may even call them superpowers," he added while trying to look like his version of a superhero. "But deep conversation is not my comfort zone."

"Humility also isn't part of your comfort zone, Horado," I said. "Although I would almost place one of two of your talents in the superpower category. Just don't get any ideas. My Mamá is sitting right here."

"I think it's time to take you out salsa dancing," Horado told me. "It's Friday night. I'm home on a weekend for a change. The children will be fine, they have tamales ready for dinner."

"Now you're talking my superpower," I said. "We've moved from soothe to enthuse."

Chapter Four

I LOVE THE SILENCE OF SATURDAY mornings. I treasure that time when the house is doing its job, protecting our family from the outside. The outside weather, the outside dangers, the outside influences of the world. Holding the inside together, inseparable, close, intimate. Family.

Horado was sleeping soundly. He wore himself out dancing last night. He needs to work out more regularly. I could tell he was overdoing it, but he wanted me to have fun, so we danced nearly every dance for two hours. I considered feigning the need to take a break, but he was working so hard ensuring I was getting to dance I didn't have the heart to stop. I did call the night short, though. I'm glad I did. It was a great evening out and an even better late-night in.

Usually, Horado starts snoring early in the morning, a couple hours before we usually get out of bed. I have learned to sleep through his *rocando como serruchos*, snoring like saws. Not just one saw mind you, but a lumber mill of saws. This morning the silence woke me up. I checked his breathing and then got up.

I went downstairs to the kitchen for some juice. Along with a thirty-minute workout every morning, I have the habit of kickstarting my systems by a cup of juice. Usually orange juice.

When I began my routine, about a year after Adelita was born, I disliked both the workouts and the juice. Now I love both.

Putting the juice pitcher back in the refrigerator, I discovered a note on the counter. It was in Adelita's handwriting. Was it here last night? Did we even go into the kitchen when we got home? I don't think so. I picked up the note and read,

Dear Mamá,

I am really having trouble with friends at school and I am not sure I will be able to finish the 6th Grade. I don't even want anything for my 12th birthday.

Besos, Adelita

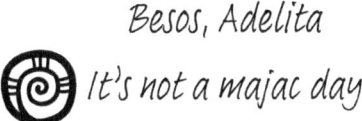 *It's not a majac day*

My immediate thought was, I shouldn't have gone dancing last night. I discarded that thought. Maybe being gone gave Adelita the space to decide to write this note. And maybe her obsession with chocolate issues was only a symptom of social problems she is having at school. Other than some Christmas wish lists and birthday cards, this is the first note Adelita had given me. It was a sad one. It didn't make logical sense, 'but why should it have to?' I asked myself. So much for the perfect Saturday morning with everyone safe and the world in its place. The world had entered our home like a virus, unseen and insidiously. Well, I had the partial antidote.

"Adelita, cariñita, are you awake?" I called up to her room. "Adelita, time to get up mija." I walked past the stairs leading up to the bedrooms and headed downstairs to the chocolate room. Usually, I had a small stash of chocolate in the kitchen, but I had shared that with Paco and Adelita earlier in the week.

I went through the laundry room, thinking I needed to get to the laundry yet this morning. I kicked Paco's old tennis shoes out of the way. They reminded me of huitlacoche, edible corn fungus, gone bad. I would probably have to throw them away. They bumped the laundry room door and it partially shut. I put in the electronic code and went into the Chocolate Room. I grabbed a couple bars and studied the room, so much to do, and then turned and left.

Instead of going directly to Adelita's room, I returned to the kitchen to put away the extra chocolate. I was surprised to see Adelita standing there, looking, a little out of breath?

"Are you feeling ill Adelita?" I asked.

"No, I'm fine," she said. "I wanted to tell you that I talked myself into a bad mood last night. This morning I felt bad that I left you that silly note. I didn't want you to feel guilty about going out with Papá last night either. Things are good at school. Really. I will move on from the drama and not let it get to me."

I started to hand her some chocolate, hoping we could talk more. "This isn't just a brave act to protect me from your challenges?" I asked, searching her face for answers.

She gave me a kiss on the cheek and left the kitchen. I stood there frozen with the chocolate in my out reached hand. Girls, or at least this girl, was more complicated to raise than my experience with boys. With Paco a chocolate bar seemed to solve most of his problems. I suspected Paco even manufactured a few problems to get a chocolate treat. I didn't mind. I tossed the chocolate on the counter and jokingly said, "Oh well, maybe Paco has a problem this morning."

It ended up being the lazy and relaxing Saturday morning I had first anticipated. We even had breakfast together. That was a treat for me. Usually, everyone is on a separate schedule and breakfast is more like a series of events as the people in my life come along the conveyor belt of time, I feed them quickly as they pass by and before I know it, they are all out the door and I wonder if they even noticed that I was standing there, usually in the kitchen, the only one not moving as they woosh by.

I noticed Horado was moving a little slow. "You okay Johnny Vazquez?" I asked him.

"Who is Johnny Vazquez?" Horado asked.

"A famous salsa dancer," I answered with a smile.

"Oh. How do you know these things?" he asked.

"He lives here in Los Angeles," I said. "How could you miss the billboards advertising his classes? He is known as the Prince of Salsa."

"I make it a point not to read billboards," Horado said. "And if he is the Prince of Salsa, then I am El Rey, the King. Not that I have all the moves, but I am married to the Queen of Salsa and that makes me the king."

"You have plenty of moves mi Rey," I said. "It appears you are moving a little slow this morning, though. Sore muscles?"

"Last night taught me I need to start again with daily workouts like you," Horado said in a surprising admission of not being perfectly fit.

"Let's go on a walk this afternoon," I suggested. "You can loosen those muscles and reduce the lactic acid in your legs."

"Do I get to hold your hand?" Horado asked.

"You get to hold my hand," I said.

"Then it's a date," he responded. And he started singing, the ballad El Rey, trying his best and failing to sound like Vicente Fernández. "*Yo se bien que estoy afuera, Pero el día que yo me muera, Se que tendras que llorar, Llorar y llorar, Llorar y llorar.*" He grabbed me and started dancing a waltz while translating the words of the song to English.

"*I know full well that you think I'm an outcast, but the day that I die—I know that you will weep. (Weep and weep, Weep and weep). You'll say that you didn't love me, but you will be filled with sadness and you're going to stay like that. With or without money, I do always what I desire and my word is law."*

"Yes, Oh King, your word is law," I sang. "Now, go upstairs and get your dirty clothes, it's royal laundry day."

Paco laughed and Adelita clapped. Horado bowed, and I gently kicked his behind. Then I bowed.

After a quick lunch of microwaved tamales Paco left to play basketball with friends. Adelita buried herself in a book. Horado and I left the house for a walk.

"Adelita wrote me a note last night while we were gone," I explained to Horado when we were out of the house. I saw it this morning. She said she was having problems with friends at school. Then when I confronted her this morning, she said everything was fine."

"What did the note say?" Horado asked.

"Trouble with friends at school, mostly," I said. "She didn't even want to have her twelfth birthday."

"But this morning you say she was fine?" he asked.

"She seemed to be herself, happy, focused on other things," I answered.

"So, everything is fine," Horado said, happy that a problem was solved.

"I'm not so sure," I said. "It felt like she had created the whole thing for a bigger reason, only to close it up only hours later."

"You said she wrote it last night?" Horado asked.

"Yes, I think so," I said. "I didn't go in the kitchen last night when we got home. I don't think she wrote it early this morning, but if my intuition is right, that is a possibility."

"You have no proof for your intuition," Horado said while making a swooshing movement with his free hand. "She wrote it last night and had a good sleep and she saw her error and rescinded her emotional action of the night before. She is grow-ing up. Maybe her wish to not have a birthday was an indirect way of saying she knows she is growing up too and doesn't want to."

"Don't reflect your own feelings on your daughter," I said. "You may not want to grow up, but your daughter sure does. She has her life practically planned out down to the exact location of every sequin on her Quinceañera dress."

"That's three years away," Horado said.

"Exactly," I said. "Adelita doesn't change her tune that fast. Something is stressing her out. I have considered her school. She says she loves it, but I don't know. This research project has her on edge. Paco had the same teacher, and it was no big deal for him."

"Está en la edad del pavo," Horado said. "It's that awkward age. Not quite a teenager, trying to figure things out. Paco still hasn't come to the crossroads of potential adulthood. He is growing, physically and mentally, but emotionally he is comfortable going with the flow. Not much shakes him, that is unless the Lakers lose a game."

"I suppose you are right," I said, feeling a little better. Changing the subject, I asked, "I haven't looked at the calendar in the last couple of days, but has Tio Ignacio suggested any delivery trips for this next week?"

"I should be home for a while," Horado said. "I explained to Tio that we are tight on supplies due to the Hurricane hitting the Yucatan. He is going to filter potential deliveries to only those of the highest priority for now."

"That's good to hear," I admitted. "I am stressed, and I can't put my finger on it. I'm glad you will be around. That will also give us some time to get our chocolate manufacturing processes better organized."

"I'm up for that," Horado said. "I thought you were going to tell me you signed me up for salsa dance lessons."

"Would you go?" I asked, knowing the answer.

"No," he replied. "I like dancing only because you like danc-ing. Dance for the art of dance is,"

"Not macho?" I interjected.

"No, it's not that," Horado replied a little too quickly. "I just don't get it. There are things I want to learn, things I want to improve in my life, but dedicating time to dance lessons, well, I know there are people better and smarter than me that dedi-cate a lot of time to that, but it's so far down my list, I could go through my entire life and be just fine without getting to that. Come to think of it, if I did get to dancing lessons on my things to improve list, that would mean I had accomplished some incredible things, so maybe I will add it to the bottom of my list."

"So, what are a few things on this list?" I asked, noticing he hardly took a breath with that explanation.

"Well, it's more of a fuzzy list," he said. "I haven't thought about it as an actual written and formal list, like a shopping list."

"But surely you have some thoughts of things you would like to learn or get better at," I pushed.

"I do want to get healthier," he admitted. "Just don't tell me dance would be a great way to accomplish that."

We walked in silence for a few minutes, enjoying the sun and the park. It was another reason, along the house and that Paco and Adelita wouldn't have to change schools, that we moved here. This park was only a block from our house. It was like our own giant backyard.

"Painting," Horado said.

"What?" I asked, being startled out of my reverie. "Painting?"

"Yeah, painting," Horado repeated, sounding slightly embar-rassed. "I would like to learn to paint."

"You mean like for a job, like painting houses?" I asked.

"No, I mean like painting pictures, or people, or things, places, I'm not sure," Horado said.

PEACE OF CHOCOLATE

"I think that is awesome, and not very macho," I said squeezing his hand.

"Painting can be macho, can't it?" He asked with a grin.

"Yes, it can," I said. "The most macho of men do whatever good things they want to do, because they aren't afraid to be authentic."

"You aren't talking about being authentic," Horado said. "You are about to launch into that power of vulnerability speech you give me about once every other month."

"Okay, maybe I was," I said laughing at his observation. "It's a great speech, admit it. It makes so much sense, right?"

"And you think admitting I would like to learn to paint isn't being vulnerable?" Horado asked. "I don't need to go around telling people I want to be open and exposed to potential ridicule."

"Don't get transparency and vulnerability mixed up," I said. "Oh, sorry, I'm preaching again. You are right, let's leave that topic and focus on painting. How did you get interested in painting? I didn't even know you liked art."

"I have never thought about it as art," Horado said. "I have been studying Tio Ignacio, his painting. It's amazing, you know? It's just some brush strokes on a canvas, but it's him. It's his face, his emotions, his life, sitting there for everyone to see."

"I don't know how that works, but you know you probably won't be painting pictures that talk back," I said, hoping I wasn't raining on his parade.

"I think there are different ways art can talk back," Horado said. "I know this interest doesn't even come close to my two other names. That's why I haven't, up until now, said anything out loud, even to myself."

"Your other names focus on goals and achievements. I don't think they are meant to be limiting in what you can or should learn or accomplish," I said. "They aren't a blueprint or a map of your life."

"I know, "Horado admitted, "but I don't think I've given enough attention to those names, and now I am thinking of other things that will take away even more time from those goals. My aspirational name, Zan, means providing support. Remember, I was given that name shortly after marrying you. I think I have done a pretty good job at that, haven't I?" Before I could answer Horado continued. "My achieved name is Cadmael and means war chief. I got that name before I really ever earned it."

"First of all," I said, stopping and turning to get eye contact with him, "you are a great provider. Our lives are not typical. You can't measure your progress by promotions in a career field or increase in salary like some corporate job. No new perks, no new toys to show off your economic prowess. I get it, it's hard to gauge how you are doing from some of the world's measures. But we just moved to a new house, an awesome house in an awesome neighborhood. Our children go to great schools and have good friends. The cultural diversity has got to be the best in the whole world. I wouldn't want to live anywhere else."

"We do live in a great place, although it can also be pretty scary sometimes," Horado said.

"I'll take our challenges over Brentwood and Beverly Hills any day," I said. "Under your wise oversight, our funding source, our family's treasure, has increased, even though we have increased deliveries by fifteen percent around the world over the past eight years. I would say you are doing amazing, not to even mention, the immeasurable good we've done in the lives of others."

"Okay, I didn't mean for this to get into a Praise and Honor Horado Hour," Horado said.

He was so cute when he got embarrassed. I shifted gears. "As for being named after a war chief, that might be a nod to your

Toltec ancestry. You know the Maya of Chichen Itza and your ancestors from Tula are connected."

"The Aztecs and many of the Maya claim descendance from Toltec nobles," Horado said. "There is the connection of the worship of Quetzalcoatl, Kukulkán to the Maya, but how do you see my name, Cadmael, war chief, given to me because of my Toltec blood?"

"Because the Toltec were the fiercest warriors of the Americas," I reminded him.

"My vote goes to the Purépecha, the Tarascans, of Michoacan," Horado said. "Neither the Aztecs nor the Spanish ever conquered them. That would have been the epic war, the Toltecs versus the Tarascans. But it never happened."

"Don't wander off my point," I said as we neared our house. "The Toltec were tough warriors. They were experts with the blow gun, as were the Mayans. You are an expert, a natural, with the blow gun."

"Some say the Toltec brought the blow gun to the Mayans," Horado said, warming to this topic. "The Toltec also brought the blow gun to the Cherokee to their north. But why not give me a name like Hunahpu after the blow gun Mayan hero? Why war chief? I feel like a charlatan, at best an aspirant."

"Don't dispute the voice of the people just because you don't understand it," I asked him. "Faith in God doesn't come from perfect understanding. If that were the case, there would be no need for faith."

"I trust God because he is God," Horado said, opening the front door for me. "I am more cautious with people because they are not God."

"No busca tres pies al gato, quit looking for three feet on the cat," I said.

"Sorry, I guess I am making this more complicated than it probably is," Horado said.

'You know," I said with a sudden insight, "The Toltecs were also famous throughout the western hemisphere as artisans. Maybe that is where your interest in painting comes from."

"Or maybe I am in a midlife crisis and looking for something new and fun to do," Horado said. "Not all our interests, talents and passion are hereditary. Our first ancestors weren't passion-less because they didn't have an ancestor to blame it on."

"Painting is a better midlife crisis choice than sports cars or swimming with sharks," I said. "You should pick up the supplies you think you need and try it out. Don't put it off. When the Toltecs had a land to conquer, they did it."

I could feel Horado's excitement about this painting idea. His dark features and strong arms and hands made him look passionate, even when he was accomplishing the mundane. He had taken on the Canul family legacy as it was his own, even down to taking the Canul name. Never looking back, becoming the best custodian of the family funds since, well, ever. I doubted his taking up painting would be a passing fad. Me on the other hand, I was more like the butterfly. I wouldn't stay long on one flower and the wind could blow me off course. I knew that about myself and I knew Horado knew that about me, even before we were married. Horado brought stability and according to him I brought spontaneity and serendipity to our marriage.

Neither of the children are exact copies of us. Paco was a little more singularly focused. That came from Horado. The rhyming thing Paco picked up on a whim—from me all the way. It will be his practice for some time if I had to guess. Adelita was more moved by the moment, as I tended to be. She had long-term goals and thoughts and was mostly willing to sacrifice to achieve her goals which reminded me of Horado.

Our children, the best and the worst of their parents? I hoped not. I hoped they were simply themselves and our job was to nurture and support the best part of their characters. It's fun, even an easy rationale for our actions, to blame them on ancestors, our environment, negative and positive influencers in our lives, how much money we have or don't have, and so on. I believed we were born with predispositions, but basically, we were also born to choose. No one could force us to be this or that way.

I was suddenly frustrated with my conversation with Horado on our walk. Do I really believe we are our own agents? If so, why did I say the things I did to Horado? I was searching for excuses for his interests and actions. Was I trying to strengthen his resolve to make a decision and take a specific course of action? Do those disingenuous means justify a good end?

Ugh, I hate conversations I knew I would revisit many times in the future. It's part of my self-diagnosed obsessive-compulsive behavior. When does pondering become rumination? I decided for myself, when it led to detachment; detachment from work, from Horado and the children. I figured I was still okay.

We found Adelita in the library. She seemed preoccupied with her school report, so I didn't bother her. As I completed the weeks laundry, Horado interrupted me.

"I just got a text from the Council," he explained. "I got a very cryptic message demanding I travel to Mexico immediately. Maybe they won't be able to supply the chocolate pods as planned. They only say they want to talk to me in person, no later than tomorrow afternoon. I tried reconnecting with them, but no answer."

Otra vez, el Palenque esta mudo," I said. "No surprise there is only silence. That seems to be their new operating procedure. I suppose you had better go. Your firsthand look at the problems they are facing after the hurricane might help us with our own planning."

"I can save some time and money by driving down to Tijuana and taking the non-stop to Merida in the morning. I can rent a car there and drive to Mayapán. I could meet with the Council by early afternoon."

"That sounds good to me," I said. "I wish this would have happened during the school break. We could take the children."

"I'm not sure this would be a good time, if Mayapán is still without power and clean water."

"Well, then we could have gone with you as far as Tijuana and stayed in Rosarito," I suggested, knowing none of these ideas were going to happen. "I hope someday we are able to use some of our funds to buy a little place on the beach down there."

"Someday, maybe," Horado said. "When we earn it. That's not what the family fund is for. As for today, I need to pack and get on the road."

Horado left right after dinner and called me when he had arrived in San Diego. He would take the Cross-Border Express to the Tijuana Airport in the morning.

"Something about this whole trip feels odd," he told me over the phone. "No real explanation in the text message, no answer when I tried to call back. Not a word from them since, attempting to confirm I am coming or when I would arrive."

"It's odd, but what has been normal with the Council over the last several months, even before the hurricane hit?" I noted. "Let me know right away if it is something I should be there for also. I can get my Mamá to come over and be with the children for a few days."

"I'll call you no matter the issue," Horado assured me. "Probably just a logistics issue with the raw pods. I'll be home in a couple days max."

I didn't hear from Horado the next day at all. It could just be the communication problems the Council had mentioned due to the hurricane damage, but I started getting worried. I tried to call his phone and didn't get an answer. I dialed the Council number. No answer. At first that made me feel a little better.

Probably just cell towers down, but why did it work when we had our video conference a few days ago? Another Hurricane? I attempted to get Tio Ignacio to talk to me. Silence. Forget what I said about loving silence. I hate it.

Chapter Five

"**H**ORADO IS FINE," THE VOICE on the other line assured me. "That is, he will continue to be fine if you work with us."

I was about to ask who this was and what was going on when I saw another call on my phone. It was another number I didn't recognize. I was going to ignore it, but instead I watched my finger click the 'hold and answer' button.

"This is Horado," this new voice said. It took me a couple of seconds to recognize it was actually him. "You are going to get a call from someone on the Council. They are going to create some crazy stories, probably some threats. Play along, but don't give them any information." I could tell Horado was running. He was out of breath and pushed out words in between gasps of breath. "I will call back later. A lot going on. Loco, muy loco. Don't call this number back. I'm tossing this phone after this call. Love you." The call went dead. I went back to the other call. That person was still talking.

"…hope you understand the serious nature of your situation. Señora? Are you there?"

"Yes, I'm here," I mumbled, trying to get my mouth to work. "Who did you say you were?" I asked.

"We, I, didn't say," the voice said. It was a female voice, middle aged, speaking English with a Yucatec Mayan accent. "I will need you to transfer the funds you have hoarded these many centuries over to an account in Panama that you will receive by text shortly. Don't try to tell me the money has been spent. I have enough information to know that significant funds remain."

"You have the ear of the Council?" I said, fishing. The only people that knew these funds even existed, let alone that it was still sufficient to run our chocolate delivery operations, were the members of the Canul Council. The Council didn't know how much, and they didn't have access to any of those funds, but they saw our basic operations reports.

"I have your ear, that is all that matters," this woman said.

"You obviously have my number," I said, trying to remain calm. "In your text repeat all that you have said. Make it clear and make it quick." I hung up. I just closed a call on someone threatening to kill my husband. I had a good idea who the caller was. "The Xiu Family," I said out loud.

"K'abel Xiu," I said. "Lady Xiu," I repeated sarcastically, "is behind this." 'Irritant or nemesis?' I thought to myself as memories flooded my mind.

"Every Ahab has his Moby Dick," Horado had said. We were young students at UNAM, the Universidad Nacional Autónoma de México.

"So, you see me as an obsessed old sea captain?" I asked Horado.

"Well, I see you more like Katniss Everdeen and K'abel Xiu as Cruella de Vil, but that is mixing stories," Horado corrected.

"Nice save," I said, "even though you might fail in a writing class, I will give you a B+."

"I don't really think she would kill puppies for a coat," Horado added, "but she has an evil elegance that I once mistook for an exotic mystique. I think she is harmless. Don't let her bother you so much."

"It took you six months dating her to see through her exotic mystique?" I asked.

"We didn't date exclusively," Horado explained. "She was a girl from home, even though I didn't know her there."

"And she's gorgeous," I admitted.

"Uniquely cute," Horado said. "Not gorgeous, not like you."

I remember, Horado said that like a fact, not trying to make points with me. I don't even think he realized it. It was like he was commenting on a sunset that everyone else could see as well. I think that might have been the moment I moved from like to love. He was a smart student, but humble. He was good looking but wasn't a player. He helped people, and it came naturally. He expected nothing in return. I liked him, a lot. I respected him and he made me a better person when I was around him. But when I was around him, I was simultaneously on solid, stable ground and in an eight-magnitude earthquake. He hadn't even kissed me for the first time when he made the gorgeous statement. I knew I was going to spend the rest of my life with him and that it would be a meaningful and passion filled journey.

And that journey would include K'abel Xiu. I thought at first, when Horado and I started dating, it was just schoolgirl jealousy of an old girlfriend. She was irritating. I was a chemistry major and she was studying political science. In my senior year, I ran for president of SOEMA, the Sociedad de Energía y Medio Ambiente, a student environmentalist club sponsored by the Engineering Department. K'abel Xiu ran against me and won. I congratulated her and she insisted I call her Lady Xiu.

"I am of royal Mayan heritage," she told me. "I can understand the plebian students here would not understand the importance of that status, but you are a Canul, and have served the Xiu for centuries."

I told her, "I don't know what time warp you live in K'abel, but that was nearly a millennium ago, and even then, I don't remember ever hearing that the Canul served the Xiu."

"I am a descendant of the Red Queen and with her blood in my veins, I have a destiny that you simply wouldn't, couldn't understand."

"Um, the Red Queen was a name given to Lady Ix Tz'akbu Ajaw by modern archeologists," I corrected. "Those same archeologists now think she wasn't even Mayan, but possibly Zapotec or Toltec."

"And she was the powerful wife of Pakal, and the grandmother of the last Mayan ruler of Palenque," K'abel added. "I'm sure Horado could fill you in on that side of her history."

"You know what, K'abel," I said, "You're loca. Is this royalty thing, and competing against me really about me taking Horado from you? I didn't, you know. He asked me out on a date and I said yes. We like each other. That's it." I remember feeling as much frustrated with myself as with her. We were both trying to nail down our identity, she with crazy claims of ancient royalty ties, and me falling in love with my stability, Horado. I felt sorry for K'abel and knew if we could ever both find ourselves, we could actually be good friends. I couldn't change her. She would have to do that. But I could work on myself. I could find my name that somehow, I misplaced years ago.

"This is only the beginning," K'abel spat, bringing me back to reality. She turned and walked away.

I hoped that was the end of our confrontations. She really was pretty, physically. Slightly plump which actually made her more beautiful. I noticed other students checking her out as she stomped away. I wondered why it had taken Horado six months to see past her appearance. Inside she was a demon with a mission.

I was shaken from my memories by my cell phone ringing. I held my breath and answered.

"Amor, it's me," Horado said. "Did someone from the Council contact you?"

"Yes," I answered. "I think it was K'abel Xiu."

"She isn't on the Council, thank goodness," Horado said with a chuckle. "Her sister is the secretary though, right?"

"Right, but that is an administrative position, not leadership," I said. "How can you laugh? I have been worried sick you were in danger, or worse."

"Worse?" Horado asked. "You mean like being captured by Lady Xiu and forced to do her bidding?"

"Keep joking like that and I will kill you myself," I said. "Where are you and what's going on?"

"Nothing new in Merida," Horado said, sounding tired now. "Some greedy members of the Council want the money. They have no interest in the mission, just filling their pockets with the claim the treasure is rightfully theirs and we have stolen it from them."

"Why is it we even put up with this ridiculous Council?" I asked. "They don't do anything to help us, especially now that we are manufacturing the chocolate. Maybe it's time to ignore them and move on. Maybe in the distant past the Council was involved in delivery or providing names the chocolate should be delivered to. But they listen to what they want to hear and provide zero oversight or support."

"The system was established in wisdom long ago," Horado said. "You were wondering how our family could have gone six hundred years without catastrophe or tragic failure? In part it's because of the thorn in our side called the Canul Council."

"Let's not get into that discussion again," I interjected. "Where are you and what is your plan to come home?"

"I'm in Panama," Horado said. "I was hungry for ceviche."

"Panama?" I repeated, ignoring his annoying lightheartedness. "Where K'abel or her sister wanted me to deposit our funds?"

"I followed one of my captors here," Horado said.

"I want to hear that story too," I said, somehow forgetting how this all started. "You landed in Merida and then what happened?"

"Remember, I didn't actually know who summoned me to Mexico, so I rented a car and drove to the Council offices."

"You make it sound like they have this suite of offices," I interjected. "Last I was there, they had a single office with a conference room adjacent to the chocolate manufacturing facility."

"Same place," Horado said. "I'm not sure what they are going to do now, since they could only pay for that place because we paid for the chocolate they made. Maybe that is what drove one or more of the Council members to team up with the Xiu family to demand our funds. I got there and it was a mess. The roof was partly blown off and the office was unusable."

"So, you think that is how the Xiu family member had the information that we still had a sizeable amount of funds, from a Canul Council member?" I asked.

"That's my guess," Horado said. "While I was poking around the manufacturing facility, thinking maybe I could offer to purchase some of their equipment and ship it to our facility, to provide them with a little cash, I was shot with a dart."

"Someone playing your game?" I said, surprised and scared. "Are you going to be okay?"

"It didn't even knock me out," Horado said lightly laughing. "It hit my wallet of all things, but it startled me. I turned to see where it had come from and someone came up behind me and put a bag over my head. I know, sounds crazy that someone could do that without me seeing or hearing them, but that's what happened. I was pushed down on a desk and another person zipped tied my hands. Honestly, it was done with such force and precision, I think it was a hired security team or maybe mercenaries."

"And that is a better story to tell yourself," I said chuckling, "that it took a professional team to take you down."

"They won the first battle," Horado said, "but I won the second one. A voice I recognized from the Council, Gerardo Diacono, told me not to struggle or they would knock me unconscious. I complied and was taken to some kind of open topped vehicle. I'll admit I thought it was an army or Federales jeep and I was in some real trouble."

"Horado, mi amor," I said, "it sounds like Diacono put you in serious danger, no matter who was carrying out his orders. I am so grateful you are safe. How did you get away?"

"It was my superior survival skills," Horado said nonchalantly, like that would be obvious to anyone. "That and the fact that they were pulled over by actual Federales. I mean, they were driving down the highway with a guy in the backseat of an open vehicle with a bag on his head. My captors were not narcotraficantes that had any crooked cops on their payroll. Maybe we got pulled over because they wanted to be on someone's payroll, I don't know."

"Did Diacono get arrested?" I asked.

"No," Horado replied. "When the Federal Office pulled the bag off my head I smiled and told him they were taking me to a bachelor party and I was getting married the next day. I admitted they had gotten a little out of control, but it was all in fun. The officer requested a refresco for his trouble and I paid him a thousand pesos, after one of Diacono's thugs cut the zip line around my hands. Get this, I was sitting in the back of one of those Volkswagen cars called a Thing. I am sure we looked ridiculous."

"Yes, incredible survival skills, Horado," I said.

"Well, it was my story," he said. "I got out of the car while the officer was still there and said I would find my own way to the party. I grabbed a taxi and Diacono followed me. Once we were back in Merida, I told my cab to continue driving while I slipped out after we turned a corner, outside of Diacono's view. I hid in a small tienda while their Volkswagen attack vehicle drove past. I purchased a cell phone and called you. I had to run to keep Diacono's car in view. I thought it would be pretty easy to follow the only Volkswagen Thing in Merida."

"How did you know they were going to demand our funds?" I asked.

"Oh, sorry, I forgot that part," Horado said. "Diacono was demanding it from me, but I told him you had the key code to the account at home. I told him we never travel with something that important and sensitive. He bought my explanation. My incredible survival skills."

"Your skills at lying through your teeth," I said smiling into the phone. I just wanted to kiss him and then punch him in the arm.

"I gave Diacono the slip and went to the airport, thinking a public place and my escape route would be the best plan," Horado continued, ignoring my astute clarification. "While I was sitting in a corner, out of view, but able to see people walking to their gates, I saw one of the thugs with Diacono. I thought they were looking for me, but they were oblivious to my presence."

"Don't say it," I said. "That had nothing to do with your incredible survival skills."

"You're right," Horado said. "I had shifted to my escape and evasion skills. Instead of coming home, I followed them to their flight, to Panama. I was able to purchase a first-class ticket, so I got on last and was off first."

"Why," I asked. "What good is it to be in Panama? What if they saw you?"

"I wanted to get Diacono on neutral ground and question him," Horado said. "He is supposed to be on our team. I don't want to be afraid to travel to our ancestral lands, to our own Council, and never know what is really happening."

"You be safe," I demanded. "We can sort this out later. You need to be here for Adelita's birthday party. Come home."

"Okay," Horado said. "If I can't get to him in the next few hours, I will catch the next flight home."

"I need you home Horado," I admitted. "That phone call shook me up. We are in the business of helping people. I know there is some danger with some of your deliveries, but not like this. People do dangerous things for money."

"Hasta pronto, mi amor," Horado said and the line went dead.

I had to force myself to breath so I wouldn't go dead.

* * *

"Lucy, I'm home," Horado yelled in his best Ricky Ricardo accent. I don't think he has ever seen an *I Love Lucy* rerun, but somehow, he picked up the entrance line years before.

I closed my eyes and said a brief prayer of thanks. I finally felt safe to leave the library. I had been sitting there trying to read a book most of the morning. I was on the same page I opened two hours ago. Without realizing it, I started to cry. That is how Horado found me. Great.

"It's okay, querida," Horado said soothingly while he stroked the hair by my neck. "I'm home. It is all over."

"What do you mean, it's all over?" I asked. "Do you mean there are no more problems with the Council or some of its rogue members? Do you mean you can tell me you, or me, or one of the children won't get kidnapped and held as a hostage ever again? Do you mean we just go on like nothing happened, like an ostrich with his head in the sand, and pretend it's over?"

"Maybe somewhere in the middle of all those options," Horado said. "I did get to talk with Diacono. I had no idea, but he lives in Panama City. He went out to eat last night. He met a couple at a restaurant. I followed him inside and sat down with him and this couple. I didn't recognize them. I told him I wanted answers. He excused himself from his table and we walked outside. He told me he was in a difficult position and didn't know where else to turn. Those people in the restaurant were his banker and her husband. That should make you feel good. The banker was the lady, and her husband was, just there. Diacono called him a hood ornament. I don't think he likes them. He is extremely late on a sizable loan. He didn't get into details and it would've sounded hollow telling him that he should've just asked for help. I know we don't make loans with the chocolate funds and I was ticked off he had threatened you."

"So, what did you do?" I asked in between sobs.

"I told him never to threaten my family, ever," Horado said, "or I would send you to deal with this just like you took care of Lady K'abel Xiu."

"You didn't," I said.

"I did," Horado confirmed, "and he actually laughed. I told him we would see what we could do to get the chocolate manufacturing at the Mexico facility back in operation as quickly as possible. I didn't say a thing about his loan issue."

"And that was it?" I asked. "You didn't punch him in the nose or something for kidnapping you and scaring your wife half-to-death?"

"I felt sorry for him," Horado said. "He is a messed-up guy, trying to make sense of his life. He is alone as far as I can tell, and maybe the only thing that brings any purpose to his life is the Council. Outwardly he is chasing money, but really, he is looking for meaning. I didn't want to give him another excuse layer as he digs down to his personal issues."

"Horado, there you go again trying to fix everybody," I said, my tender emotions being replaced by a harder anger. "He doesn't get a free pass just because his actions were motivated by some sad issues. Napoleon didn't get a get out of jail free card after plundering Europe just because he was short. The Spanish can't excuse their ruthless conquering of this continent just because they had some left-over soldiers of fortune after kicking the Moors from Iberia who repurposed themselves as conquistadores. He made decisions and there are consequences. I know we aren't his judge and jury, but we don't just let this go."

"I know, I know, but there is more," Horado explained. "He told me that we had bigger problems and that I was only seeing *ni la mitad de la historia,* only the tip of the iceberg. What do you think that means?"

"Someone else has designs on the funds, I guess," I said. "Is all this worth it? Could we give up half of the money to the Council, close it down and quietly disappear?"

"Quitting something that truly makes a difference is not the answer. Yes, querida, it is all worth it," Horado said, now kissing my neck. "We will figure this out." Changing the subject, Horado asked, "Are we ready for Adelita's party?"

I slugged Horado in the arm which I knew would only make my hand sore. "I'm the genetic Canul. Where do you get this passion for our mission?"

"Doing good is not genetic," Horado said smiling. "Doing good comes from feeling the sun and turning your face toward it. When the day becomes colder, the warmth of the sun is even more glorious."

"And when night comes?" I asked.

"And at night, we go dancing because we have done what we could and it is our turn to stand and show that we can go forward on our own," Horado said. "And if a few doubts creep in while the music isn't playing, we remember that the sun is there, just around the corner. It will warm us again if we choose not to stay in the shadows."

"Dancer and a poet," I said giving him a well-deserved kiss. "It isn't time for dancing, but it's time for Adelita's party. She wants to get tacos."

"Tacos El Güerro on Atlantic Boulevard?" Horardo asked, his mouth already salivating. Amazing how he could shift from introspective philosopher to little boy faster than you can say tacos al pastor.

The birthday party was a success. I felt better seeing my family fill their stomachs with carne asada, and contentment. Adelita loved getting the microscope she had hoped for and her abuela gave her a note and a family heirloom necklace. Her abuela, my Mamá, was not feeling well and couldn't make it to the party, but I will take Adelita to visit her soon.

"How much longer will we have my Mamá with us do you think?" I asked Horado later that night.

"Many, many years," Horado said. "Speaking of Abuela, I was considering trying to paint her portrait as my first live subject. What do you think?"

"Maybe take a few photos of her and paint from that," I suggested. "I'm not sure she would want to sit for too long in one position. I think she would be honored."

"It just seems appropriate to start with the family matriarch," Horado said getting into bed. "I fear it won't be very good, but if there is one person who would be understanding about that, it would be her. I could try to paint you first, but I want to get more experience before I try for my masterpiece."

"I am to be your masterpiece?" I asked as I snuggled into bed beside him.

"You are already God's masterpiece," Horado said putting his arm around me. "I just want to do His creation justice, even in my imperfect mortal way."

"You just did, mi amor," I said as I closed my eyes to one of those near perfect days. It was times like these when I felt my name was within my reach. I held my identity in my heart. Sometimes, later at night I would wake up to my doubts. 'No, I am holding my identity with my arms around my husband. Is there a me independent of others? Is that a bad thing to think? Does it matter? I am happy and love my life. Why this self-centered concern over myself like I was a tiny island in the vast ocean? I was a protected and verdant valley surrounded by guardian mountains on all sides, or part of an archipelago of amazing islands. Yet, I knew, in order to nurture our interdependent companionship, I needed to be more independent than dependent. I feared I wasn't offering my whole self to our union, to our children, or to my life. I breathed in my blessings, grateful for my place in the world, for my roles that brought meaning to every breath I took, and the hope that my identity was there, just not discovered yet. I gave Horado a kiss on the cheek. I closed my eyes to the day and to my doubts.

Chapter Six

"MAMÁ," ADELITA ASKED ME THE next morning, "I don't understand Abuela's note. Can you tell me what it means?"

"Let me see it," I requested. I read it aloud.

Feliz cumpleaños Adelita! You are a young lady now. With that comes new blessings, a new name, and new responsibilities. Seeds that were planted hundreds of years ago will become a part of your life someday soon. You will know when you are ready.

 *Con amor, Tu Abuela*

"Does any of that have to do with the necklace she gave me?" Adelita added. She handed me the necklace.

"The stone on the end of this necklace is jade, from our ancient homeland," I explained. "That is the family swirl carved into it."

"That's the same swirl you put on all your notes to us, isn't it," Adelita said in realization. "But what does the note mean?"

"It looks a lot like the note that my grandmother gave me when I turned twelve." I said. I was suddenly overcome with my own memories and gave Adelita a hug.

"Wait, Mamá there has to be more," Adelita said. "Abuela knows I love seeds and I already have a name. I got the love of seeds and my name from her. So, what is she talking about? New name, new responsibilities, old seeds, and deciding something? More mysteries. I'm twelve now. I need answers."

"One day you will understand it," I said with a teary-eyed smile. "Until then, be patient and know that tomorrow will be a *majac* day."

I had wanted to say so much more. Yet, after the kidnapping of Horado and Diacono's veiled caution that there was much more going on that could impact our lives, I never wanted her to know any of the family history or our mission. I knew that wasn't fair to her, or our family legacy. I hoped Horado and I were raising her and Paco to handle the burden of knowledge, even if neither chose to follow in the family profession.

Later that day I confronted Adelita's abuela. "Mamá," I asked, "I thought you were going to help open the door to our family history, not add more mystery."

"Did Adelita like the necklace?" Mamá asked.

"She loved the necklace," I said. "You aren't going to get away with answering my question with a question. Even I had to think about the note. It's worthy of a Sherlock Holmes novel."

"Thank you, chiquitita," Mamá said with a smile.

"Enough with avoiding my question," I said. "What did you mean by your note? Adelita asked me and I didn't know how to answer it without explaining everything. I am not sure I want Adelita, or Paco, to know everything. All your note did was frustrate your granddaughter."

"Seeds are a mystery wrapped in hope," Mamá said. "We all should collect seeds just like our minds collect stories. Stories are seeds that will sprout in good ground. Seeds are stories so far untold. Seeds are adventure waiting to happen if we are courageous enough to plant them."

"Plant stories then," I replied. "Don't plant conundrums a child can't solve."

"What is cunundun?" Mamá asked.

"Don't get off the subject," I countered. "Honestly, did you and Horado take the 'How to talk in riddles class' together?"

"Don't work yourself into a frenzy," Mamá said chuckling. "Adelita is much smarter than you give her credit. The seeds are planted. Give her some time. When the time comes, those seeds will open to the stories you will need to share, and they won't come as quite the shock they might otherwise be. She will not see the stories as a secret kept from her, but a secret discovered."

"A conundrum is a confusing and hard to define challenge," I said. "I don't think there is a translation in Spanish. It's not una adivinanza, a riddle, but that is as close as I can come."

"Riddles are made to be solved," Mamá said. "Now, tell me about Horado's recent adventure."

I shared most of the details, leaving out the Diacono's threat to our future. Mamá laughed and told me stories of the Council in her day. They sounded very much like our present challenges. I wondered for the hundredth time why we stayed in this business, how our family had stayed true to the cause for hundreds of years. I returned home no more certain of what I should do than when I left. It was unusually quiet when I stepped into the kitchen. I walked into the living room. No one. I jogged up the stairs to the children's' bedroom and then up to the library, empty. I wasn't surprised Paco was gone. He had said he was gong to play basketball with friends. Adelita is almost always home. I stopped by Paco's room and grabbed his dirty clothes that had miraculously found their way into his hamper.

As I reached the bottom of the stairs leading to the laundry room, I heard Paco say to someone, "No, like Papá always says, 'even a blind hog gets an acorn every once in a while.'"

It took me a moment to realize he was talking to Adelita. I was surprised they were in the laundry room. That would be a first for Paco. I heard Adelita reply as I peeked through the laundry room door, "Paco, maybe this was the secret workshop of a mad scientist who used to have a secret laboratory here before we moved into this house. Maybe this is connected to someone else's house and we aren't supposed to know about this."

"Stop the stress, you're a mess. This is connected to our laundry room—so lay off the gloom and doom," Paco said as he walked to the nearest shelf for a closer look. With an excitement that equaled my nervousness at their discovery, Paco happily observed "I've never seen this much chocolate in one place. This is something I can embrace."

I knew it was time to intervene. I mustered my courage and said in a stern voice, "This you can't embrace if I send you to outer space. Turn around so we're face-to-face."

I could tell Adelita almost fainted. Paco grabbed her and together they turned around, expecting to see something other than me. A mad scientist, The FBI? They saw me standing in the doorway and I wasn't smiling.

Neither Paco nor Adelita said a word. I couldn't imagine what was going through their minds. Looking past them into the chocolate room, I could hardly believe it. I didn't say a word, as my mind considered what to say, how much to say.

Breaking the tension, Paco said, "Hey Mamá, you're no poetic bomb. Space rhyme—a new paradigm."

I tried to look serious with my arms crossed as my heart melted. I loved these two innocent children, who weren't children anymore. The hiding and guarded truths had been uncovered. Just as Horado and Mamá had predicted, we would know when it was time to open the door to our family mission. They had opened the door. I didn't acknowledge Paco's rhyme. It seemed the seconds were expanding into hours. I saw Adelita look at my fingers on my left-hand fidgeting. I was turning my wedding ring around on my finger with my thumb. I always did that when I was pondering important decisions.

"This could be bad news," I heard Adelita whisper to Paco. "Mamá only fidgets with her ring when she is thinking hard."

That did it for me. I couldn't hold back the relief, the joy and hard times of future adventures together. I exercised my zygomaticus major muscle and broke into a big smile which made me feel a lot better, but I could tell both Paco and Adelita still felt unsure of what was going to happen.

"Don't look too startled. I had to do something with the chemical engineering degree I got in college," I said.

Both Paco and Adelita were still speechless. I noticed Adelita had been holding her breath and was actually turning pale. She took a breath just as I reached her, afraid she was going to pass out.

"But Mamá, what is this room—this is epic! This is bigger than Wal-Mart. My whole school could fit in here. Well maybe they wouldn't want to fit in here if they knew you were a mad scientist." Adelita said as words just poured out of her mouth. "Where did all this come from? Did you really build this room? How did you do it with no one noticing? Why did you do it? I am so sorry to come in here without asking. It was an accident, really..."

"Slow down Adelita. One question at a time. Since I am the Mamá here, I get to ask the first question: how exactly did you two find this room?" I asked as I looked at both of them.

Paco had his mouth full of chocolate, but he tried to say something that sounded like, "My bad, hey this candy is rad..."

"I did it Mamá," Adelita interrupted. "I saw you go into the laundry room and disappear. I was just trying to figure out where the chocolate smell was coming from. When you magically produced a chocolate bar the other day when I wrote that note I thought maybe you were hiding some chocolate somewhere in the house. I didn't exactly connect the laundry room to the chocolate smell until I saw this," Adelita said as she pointed to the shelves of chocolate. "I wasn't as observant as Paco," she admitted. "He found the keypad behind the boxes on the shelf. I figured out the password. It wasn't very hard—you write it on all your notes. I just had to change the order of the letters."

"I'm impressed!" I said. "So, you never broke the Ajmac code, you just guessed it might work? And you still figured out that it was the password for the Chocolate Room."

"The code? The Chocolate Room?" Adelita asked, obviously still confused. She wanted to say more, but then clamped her mouth shut.

"Ajmac is the password, but also a code. Maybe you can figure it out after I explain a few things. While you are wondering about that, I will answer your questions about the room." I grabbed a chocolate bar and took a bite. "This is so fun eating candy with you two in the Chocolate Room!" I added with a giggle.

Paco took that as an opportunity to grab another chocolate bar. "That is your last bar for today Paco," I stated trying to mix a little firmness with a smile.

After finishing another bite of chocolate, I said, "When we were shopping for a new house to expand our work, I was visiting the laundry room—something you both could do a little more in the future by the way. I noticed there was a piece of loose paneling here where you found the entrance. I was trying to fasten it back in place when I felt cold air coming from behind the wall. Your Papá and I took down the panel and there was this partial cavern left over from the construction of the house and the road above. You know we were the last house to be built in this area and the builder actually died before the house was fully completed. Your Papá and I decided not to tell anyone about this space in case it would cause the house to be condemned." I took another bite of chocolate as I turned to look at the room. "I expanded and built the room a little each day while you were at school— with a little help from your Papá."

"You're very handy, but why the candy?" asked Paco with a smile and a bit of chocolate on the corner of his mouth. As an afterthought he added, "Not that I'm complaining, but it's got my curiosity straining." I took out a tissue from my jeans pocket and wiped his mouth while he smirked.

"Discovering this giant cavern sold us on the house," I said. "We were expecting to find a house with a garage or some other room we could relocate our family work."

"Our family work?" Adelita asked. "That's the second time you said that."

I was obviously not prepared to explain all this. All the time I spent worrying about whether, or when to share this, I should have been practicing how to say it. I took a deep breath and asked, "What is one thing that helps people get through problems?"

Both Paco and Adelita shouted, "Chocolate!"

I guess I had done some things right in preparing them for this. "Exactly," I answered. "That is our family business."

"We sell chocolate?" Adelita asked. Her cute little face was contorted, but her big brown eyes were sparkling.

"Not exactly," I said. "First, let me explain the room. Then I will explain why we built the room. I started filling shelves with the chocolate we make. Pretty fast, I had a shelf full, but the more problems there were in the world, the more chocolate I thought we should have."

"Chocolate's great—no complaint. But from chocolate elf to making it yourself?" Paco interjected pointing to all the pots and machines.

"Ever since my college chemistry days I have been interested in chocolate. Like you, Adelita, I got a letter from my Abuela when I turned twelve. It was a mystery to me what it meant. My Abuela passed away before I could convince her to explain her words to me. Seeds? Another name? Crazy, right? But it would be years later before I discovered our family mission."

I continued, seeing I was saying too much and not enough simultaneously. "It wasn't until I started tinkering with melting slabs of chocolate and studying the chemistry of the chocolate making process, that my Mamá, your Abuela, shared with me our family work. With your Abuela's help, before I knew it, I had a small chocolate factory running in your Papá's warehouse when we lived in our old house."

"I never smelled the chocolate there," Adelita said, partly to herself. She said that like it was a failure on her part.

"You weren't ready yet," I said. "I wasn't ready until I was in college. Eventually it all works out, and for me it grew into this." I waved my hand at the chocolate room that even I still couldn't believe was real.

"The cool, but not so cold temperature, dry air, and the darkness down here keep the chocolate in good shape," I added as I pointed to the shelves of candy.

"You learned about chocolate in chemistry class?" Paco asked.

"Now that is a class I could pass," he added enthusiastically.

"It wasn't a class, it was my Abuela and then your Abuela, and that line of knowledge and understanding goes back at least 600 years. But let's wait for your Papá to get home so we can share this with you both as a family."

I walked out of the chocolate room. Paco and Adelita reluctantly followed me and as soon as we were safely out, I clapped my hands together once, paused and then clapped twice faster, to activate the sound sensor and the door began to close.

"Security is important," I said. "Your Papá and I will explain that too."

"I breathe a chocolate sigh as I have to say goodbye," Paco said as the door finished closing.

I noticed Adelita glance at the blue light blinking as we left the laundry room. She was smiling for the first time since I had discovered them in the Chocolate Room.

I called Horado when Paco and Adelita turned their attention to other things. "It happened, just as you and Mamá predicted," I said.

"What is it we predicted?" Horado asked. "If it happened, I can only say I told you so."

"Funny Horado," I said. "Adelita deciphered the code to the Chocolate Room. She opened the door and they stepped into the darkness."

"Querida," Horado said soothingly, "you make it sound like they discovered dead bodies or a lab that clones babies. It's a room that makes chocolate."

"And it opens the door to our family heritage and burden," I said. "Horado, we have to tell them now and that changes everything."

"You're right, now I can use Paco for some of the heavy lifting here at the warehouse," Horado said. "And Adelita can get involved in the chocolate production. This is great!"

"You are saying this to get under my skin," I said. "It isn't going to work. You need to come home as soon as you can. In the meantime, think about how we are going to share this with them, and maybe just as important, what we aren't going to share with them."

"Well, they don't need to know about the Council, and how they work with us," Horado said. "They don't need to know about my recent trip and that some are trying to get the funds for their own uses. Actually, they don't even need to know about the previous chocolate production process in Mexico. It seems if we focus on ancient Mexico and leave out modern-day Mexico, we can leave all these issues for another time, when they are older."

"I like that, I think," I said, my head still reeling with how to organize this explanation. "What do we say first? Every time I run through this in my head, I think, Oh, I should have explained this or that other issues first."

"Let's start at the beginning," Horado said. "It will flow just fine from there. And if there is anything we forget; we can add that later. This isn't a graded test. And we need to present it with a smile. We need to be excited about finally getting to share this with them. They need to know they earned this disclosure. It wasn't something we were going to hide from them forever, only until they were ready."

"I am glad you will be here," I admitted. "I admit I am excited to hear you explain all this."

"You are the one who should take the lead," Horado said. "I am married into this family, but you are a Canul by bloodline. This is your family history; their family history."

"And your family history," I added. "Both by blood as a Mayan and by marriage. You are to cleave unto me and we are to be one, remember."

"I will be there to back you up," Horado said. "I will leave as soon as I finish processing the paperwork to receive our first shipment of raw cacao pods."

Less than two hours later Horado walked in the door. It had seemed like two days. I was so anxious about finally telling the children about our family mission that I felt nauseous and thought for sure I would throw up, and almost did when Horado entered the house. I was up in my bedroom, trying to get my emotions under control. I didn't hear Horado come in. I felt his confidence and enthusiasm half a minute before I heard him call for me.

"I'm home," Horado called. "Anybody here?"

I heard Paco say, "Home at last, now let's hear about family past."

I took a deep breath, nodded to my reflection in the mirror and started down the stairs.

I knew Adelita was up in the library talking to Tio Ignacio. I wondered if he would ever be talking to Adelita, or perhaps Paco. Not for the first time I missed hearing Tio Ignacio's voice in my mind. I wondered what the criteria was that he, or whomever orchestrated Tio's communications, used to decide who we would talk to, and how Tio got his information. Was he acting solo or was he just a mouthpiece for someone else? How did it work? I had always supposed there was some kind of science behind this unexplainable phenomenon. I wish I could just chalk it up to magic as Horado and my Mamá did. Here I was, about to share all this with my children and I could hardly understand it myself. I wouldn't believe it if I hadn't experienced it. Yet, I knew Adelita and probably Paco, would accept all this as natural and find it simply exciting, rather than a burden and unexplainable.

I consciously exercised my facial muscles again and felt it pull my mouth sideways and up. I waited until that movement connected to my heart. Then it became a real smile. I left the stairwell and gave Horado a hug, truly grateful he was home.

Chapter Seven

I HEARD PACO AND HORADO TALKING as I entered the living room, "Adelita asked Tio Ignacio if the swirl on her necklace and Mamá's notes were the responsibility part of Abuela's note to her. She told me she had never noticed the swirl on Tio Ignacio's coat before today. I told her it had always been there. She is nervous, Papa," Paco said. "Kind of like how Mamá gets. She is worried if we will have to keep all this a secret and she is afraid Adelita won't be able to keep whatever you share with us to herself."

So Paco knew I got nervous? He seemed so checked out when it came to family dynamics. I should never underestimate him. He is his father's son.

"Where is Adelita?" Horado asked.

"Upstairs in the library," I said as I entered the room. "Paco would you run up and get her?" I asked, hoping to get a minute alone with Horado to share notes.

"That's okay," Horado said. "Let me go get her." Horado left the room before I could say anything to change his mind. Suddenly a conversation entered my mind and I recognized both voices.

"So, this is all a big secret?" Adelita asked.

"Yes and no Adelita. That you keep it here and who you are is a secret, the chocolate is to share. You must share…" I knew that voice from long ago. It was Tio Ignacio.

"Adelita," Tio Ignacio's voice whispered again in her ear. "Adelita, it's time." Adelita opened her eyes and saw Tio Ignacio, no. In my mind's eye I could see her rub her eyes and the face of her Papá, my Horado, came into focus.

"I thought you were Tio Ignacio," She said with a yawn.

"I'm old," Horado said, "but not that old. Wake up and come downstairs. Your Mamá and I have some things to share with you and Paco."

I kept my smile, but a tear followed gravity to my chin before I wiped it away. It was so good to hear Tio Ignacio, even if just for a few words. It would all be okay. I knew it. Adelita was downstairs before Horado probably had left the library.

"Hey Adelita, you're as fast as a cheetah. It's time for family history to solve the mystery," Paco said.

Adelita sat next to Paco and turned to look at us both. Horado sat down and smiled. He looked at me, nodded and then turned back to Paco and me.

I felt like I was about to tell little children that Santa Claus wasn't real, but Martians were. I took a deep breath and let it out. "I want to start with some family history. Great, many greats, Abuela Canul," I began, "lived in what is now southern Mexico, over six hundred years ago. She was a Mayan princess. She had nine brothers. They were the guardians of the Ka'kau. The Canul brothers, they were called the Canulo'ob, lived in the city of Mayapán."

"Wait," Adelita interrupted. "What or who was Ka'kau?"

"It sounds like what it is," I answered. "Cacao. Chocolate."

"Chocolate they guarded?" Paco asked, seeming to forget to rhyme. Mom waited. Paco smiled and added, "A duty highly regarded."

"The Canul brothers were respected but also greatly feared by the nobles because of their power. The Canul brothers were banished, sent away from Mayapán and were not allowed to intermarry with the royal line any longer. Not long after, in 1461, the great city of Mayapán was decimated by an epidemic. The Canul brothers had been protected because they had been sent away. Later they each married into the royal family Xiu. They survived the Spanish conquest of Mexico and their families still live in Yucatan, Mexico to this day."

"But what about great, many greats, Abuela Canul?" Adelita asked, absorbing every word.

"Ah, this is our family line," I said. "Abuela's brothers were the guardians of the Ka'Kau, but Abuela was the keeper of the secrets of this magical plant and of Chokola'j. That is a Mayan word that means 'to drink chocolate together.' You see, the ancient Mayans believed that God gave chocolate to humans when they were created. God gave chocolate to humans to create space."

"Create space?" Adelita asked.

"I will get to that in a minute," I said. "You need to know first that we are the Canul. You Paco and Adelita, you are both Canul," Mamá repeated, looking at us. "It is more than a last name, it is our calling, our blessing and sometimes it may feel like a burden. Your direct line has always maintained the last name Canul."

It looked like Adelita had another question, but Horado spoke up. "Your first names also tell part of this story," he said. "Paco is a Spanish nickname for Francisco, but we did not name you Francisco. Your name comes from the word Pakal who was a Mayan king. His name meant 'shield' and that is your heritage. Like the ancient Canul brothers, you are a guardian."

"Proclaim a name to frame the game," Paco said. "If that's the aim, I won't cause shame."

"Someday you are going to run out of rhymes, when your wisdom exceeds your vocabulary," Horado said. "Until then, I'll just say amen. And what do you guard? Your Mamá told you about the nobles fearing the Canul Brothers, right? Over the centuries, the nobles, that is a group of rich and prideful Mayans that claimed connection to the royal family, developed into a secret group that today finds and sells Mayan artifacts. They think we may have some of those, so we are always cautious."

"And Adelita," I added getting back to the names, "You already know your name means royal, young royal. The ancient Mayans had three names. Their first was their given name. Like Adelita, Mayan princess. In fact, as a Canul you are of a royal bloodline. The second name was the *name of intent*, sort of like a goal, but it can also be a fictitious name if you choose not to accept its responsibilities. Your second name is Naylay. That means girl with perception."

"Pakal and Naylay," Horado said. "Those aren't names we will call you by, but they should be held in your hearts."

"You said there are three names?" Adelita asked.

"The third name is the *earned name*," Horado said. "That name will come in time."

"And, what was the secret great, many greats Abuela held?" Adelita asked.

"Many secrets, Adelita," I said. "Cacao is a seed. It grows on a tree that lives in humid and hot places."

"So that is why Abuela always talks to me about seeds," Adelita said, happy to solve a small mystery.

"That's right Adelita," I said. "To know and understand seeds is part of your needed perception. The ancient Mayans were the first in the world to cultivate cacao. The first to discover how to make it into chocolate. Where the ancient Mayans lived it was hot, but usually dry and the land was mostly limestone, not good soil for growing. The Canul Abuelas knew how to grow the cacao trees in cenotes. Cenotes are sinkholes that are found in the Yucatan area of Mexico. They are like tiny valleys and they have deep pools of water. It is very humid in these tiny valleys. The soil was nurtured by the Canul Abuelas and cacao trees thrived in these places. The chocolate from these valleys was sacred and not originally grown to sell and make money."

"So that is the secret?" Adelita asked. "To know how to grow chocolate?"

"Not just how to grow chocolate, but how to use it," I said. Turning to Paco I added, "And how to protect it." Then looking at us both, I explained, "A minute ago, I mentioned Chokola'j, 'to drink chocolate together.' Here is the magic of chocolate and our family duty. Six hundred years ago, this was not a secret. Now it is a secret in plain sight. There are ancient Mayan drawings carved in stone that share the secret. Kauil was the Mayan fire god, the example of decisions, both good and bad. Many carvings show his mouth open with a plate of offerings. Those offerings are usually drawn as cacao."

I smiled at Adelita and continued. "Chocolate creates a space. Before I share with you what that means, let's have some chocolate." Mamá grabbed a small paper sack I hadn't noticed by the foot of her chair and produced four chocolate bars with the swirling circle on them.

"This is special chocolate. It is called Ka'Kau Nah" I said. "That means 'the mother chocolate' in Mayan. The world calls it criollo cacao—the pure or original chocolate. Other types of chocolate create space too, but this is special chocolate that is only grown in the cenotes of the Yucatan in Mexico. I thought we should share it together on this day of mysteries solved."

Horado added, "We send our chocolate all over the country, and the world. This Mother Chocolate is for special occasions or special emergencies."

I could tell both Paco and Adelita were surprised and appreciated the special chocolate. For me it remains the best chocolate I ever tasted. We talked as a family about all that we had so far shared, and it felt good.

"Let's take a break from all this information," Horado suggested. "There is more to share, like the chocolate space your mother mentioned, but I am hungry and I don't want to fill up on chocolate."

"I agree," I said. "Chocolate can be healthy, but not in large amounts. Is this a pizza night?"

"Pizza, hunger's analgesia," Paco shouted with enthusiasm.

We enjoyed dinner together and the children went off to their own activities. Adelita buried herself in a book and Paco left for some night basketball in a neighbor's driveway.

"We are alone," Horado said. "I think that went really well. You did a good job of boiling down six-hundred years of family history."

"We hardly scratched the surface," I said. "Give them time to think about what we shared and they are going to have six-hundred questions. It did feel good, though. Thank you for your support. That was brilliant bringing up their first names. I hadn't even thought of that. It personalized the entire experience tonight. I admit I was surprised they didn't ask us about our first second and third names and the stories that go with them. I'm not sure I am ready to share that with them."

"That was a long time ago," Horado said with a smile. "I am sure most have forgotten about that."

"Everyone, but the Xiu family," I said. "I was young, overly protective, and honestly that wasn't me. I have to live with a name that isn't me Horado."

"Your idea to give them some of the Ka'Kau Nah, the mother chocolate was the best part of the night," Horado said, changing the subject. "Far beyond names, they will always associate their first insight into their family history with their first taste of the most unique and pleasing taste on the planet."

"I remember the first time I tasted Ka'Kau Nah," I said. "My Abuela gave me some. It was when my father passed away. I was a little younger than Adelita. It was a very hard time for all of us. I can't imagine what my Mamá was going through. That started our plans to move to the United States. All that change and what I remember most is the taste of that chocolate."

"Is that why you call your Papá father?" Horado asked. "I know I have asked you that before, but you have always answered with a shrug."

"I don't know," I admitted. "I have good memories of him, but also some hard memories."

"Hard memories?" Horado asked gently. "Bad memories?"

"Not bad like he hurt us or yelled at us," I said, trying to get to the bottom of this myself. "He was stern, but he was not home very much and when he was, I always tried to figure out which one was present. Sometimes he was nice, even jovial. Other times he was quiet, even sullen, or depressed. In those days, in our village anyway, no one talked about mental health. He provided for us as best he could, I think. I have guessed he suffered from some mental illness. Mamá loved him, but she told me once, during a vacation from the university, that she had not allowed my father into her bed after I was born. That's why I am an only child. That conversation was the last we ever spoke about him. You know, I don't even know how he died."

"You turned out perfect," Horado said kissing my cheek. "If that is all your mother's doing, she should be a saint. But I am guessing that your father had a part to play in those early years of your life. He was a good man I think."

"I want to believe that," I admitted. "I have no idea if he was ever very much involved in the family chocolate efforts. As far back as I can remember it was my Abuelos, my grandparents, and my Mamá. It was my father who was the Canul. My Mamá took on the family role like you have, making it her personal responsibility and passion."

"In the photo you have of him," Horado noted, "He is standing by the family's ancient chocolate manufacturing equipment. He looks proud, and his eyes look kind."

"Maybe you can get more out of my Mamá than I have been able to glean," I said, shrugging my shoulders. "Let's close that subject. What more do we share with the children?"

"They are already expecting to hear about chocolate space," Horado said. "Adelita had a lucky guess about the password to the Chocolate Room, so you could talk about that. What about Tio Ignacio, how we fund our operation, and the part the Council plays, even if we don't bring in the dynamics of the Council and the threats to taking the family funds?"

Let's leave out all of that except the chocolate space and Ajmac," I said. "Maybe my little reminder, 'itza majac day' and the swirl. That is more than I got when I was brought into the family mission, and I was a university graduate."

"I think Tio Ignacio has been talking to Adelita," Horado said. "When I went to get Adelita from the library, she had been napping, but she thought I was Tio Ignacio when I was waking her up. I asked him, before I followed Adelita downstairs, but he didn't answer."

"Let's cross that bridge if and when he talks to her or Paco," I suggested. "Would he start talking to a little girl rather than you?" I thought about what I had heard but didn't mention it. Would he use a twelve-year-old instead of an adult? I realized Horado was talking, and I pulled my thoughts back to our conversation.

"I have no idea," Horado admitted. "Maybe sometime this next week I would like to take Paco to the warehouse and have him help me. Maybe you could have Adelita help you out with manufacturing efforts in the basement. I don't want to get them too involved. But it would be a tangible connection to all this information, plus it would be healthy to be with them and help them feel the familia in the family business."

I could use Adelita's help," I said. "Maybe you could involve Paco in some deliveries. He could even travel with you during the summer. We already have their passports."

"Great idea," Horado said. "I could take him," Horado began and was interrupted by his phone. It looked like he was going to ignore it, but he looked at the caller ID and frowned. "It's the Council. I suppose I should take it."

"Hello," Horado said. His eyebrows raised and he said, "Just a minute. My wife is here. I'm going to put you on speaker." He did so and said, "Now repeat that."

The voice I recognized as Jorge Canul said, "Gerardo Diacono has resigned from the Council. As you know, when a member resigns, it is that person's prerogative to nominate their replacement for the Council to vote on. He nominated K'abel Xiu."

"Did Gerardo fill you in on his attempted kidnapping of me just a few days ago?" Horado asked.

"Kidnapping? He said there had been a misunderstanding about some financial dealings and felt bad that you had traveled to Mexico to take care of them, but that is all," Jorge said.

"I met with him in Panama, after he threatened my family and me to get access to our family funds," Horado said. "He suggested that his little power play was only the tip of the iceberg. What's going on?"

I trusted Jorge. He is my cousin. But I was surprised Horado brought up this subject with him.

"I don't know what Gerado was specifically talking about," Jorge said. "There are several subterfuges going on; one inside the Council and who knows what's going on outside our little group. I did hear the Nobles are rattling their sabers again. I don't know if Gerardo Diacono was involved with that but suggesting K'abel Xiu sit on the Council could be connected. The Nobles have several plans, and they will require funds to make them happen."

"There has not been a Xiu on the Council for more than two-hundred years," I interjected. "The last time that happened things did not turn out well."

"There is no rule against their participation," Jorge said. "I don't think she has the votes, but I wanted to warn you just the same."

"Consider us warned," Horado said. "Diacono probably doesn't have any close connection with K'abel Xiu or the Nobles. He was possibly getting paid to nominate her in order to service his personal debts. We have talked in the past of increasing the stipend the Council members receive. I have been opposed to that in the past because it tips our hat to the reality of our funds. It sounds like that secret is now common knowledge. Is it time to increase the stipend and perhaps solidify our support?"

"I doubt you could buy any new support," Jorge said, "and those who support you aren't doing so for the money. I will admit the cost of travel and the opportunity loss of what Council members could be doing instead of supporting your operations plays a role in the mood of our meetings."

"Horado and I will talk about a potential raise," I said, frowning at Horado to keep him quiet. "We will get back to you on that. Should we be worried about Lady K'abel Xiu?"

"She is a lot of noise," Jorge said. "I don't think there is much bite and you do have the Xiu's over a barrel. That agreement on the cenote ownership transfer is still valid isn't it?"

"Still valid," Horado said.

"And considering your history with K'abel in particular, I wouldn't lose any sleep over this board nomination thing. I'm sorry to bother you with all this. The Council is supposed to be a support and an advocate, not your arch nemesis."

"Opposition is a good thing," Horado said. "Sometimes that is the best support. It keeps us thinking, cautious, and in the details of our operations. That being said, we greatly appreciate the level head and positive support you have always been for us."

"As always, Horado," Jorge said, "you offer a ray of clarity and sunshine in an otherwise complex and dreary world. It is good to talk with you both. I see the raw cacao pods got to you. The manufacturing is going okay?"

"We are up and running with plans to increase output soon," I said. "Could you send a small shipment of Ka'Kau Nah pods?"

"I will see what I can do," Jorge said. "A lot of damage here, but our ancestors knew what they were doing. No damage at all in the cenotes, thus no damage to the mother trees or their pods. Un fuerte abrazo."

After Horado hung up I said, "I trust Jorge, but I was surprised you shared all that with him."

"Nothing is a secret down there," Horado said. "I bet he knew the whole story about Diacono and that he knows more about the Nobles. Sharing information with him, trusting him, is the currency, not the stipend the Council members get. We, on the other hand, are out of the loop and need Council members on our side. I have been thinking. We need actual eyes and ears that are fully trusted and proactive living down there that can keep us apprised. Is Jorge that guy? If not who?"

"So much energy dedicated to so little progress," I said. "And it is mostly because of money. We could do this job better if we didn't have all that money. It is a safety net, but it feels more like a handicap."

"You know, that is a brilliant idea," Horado said. "Let me think about that for a few days. Maybe we need a catastrophic event."

"Yes, that's just what we need," I said, rolling my eyes.

Chapter Eight

OUR NEW NORMAL FELT A lot like the old normal. I am not sure what I was expecting after having shared some family history and our mission to share chocolate with people. Adelita was still in grade school and read books both for school and enjoyment. Paco still played basketball after school. I was still their Mamá and Horado still helped me feel safe. I still worried about the pressures of all this on the children. I thought some of that stress or anxiety would dissipate. If anything, it had increased. I looked for warning signs in Adelita especially, that she was feeling overwhelmed, or extra moody. She appeared as resilient and contented as always.

It was special being able to share chocolate-making with Adelita and I know Horado was enjoying having Paco at the warehouse now and then. Things were good. Things were not good. I admitted to myself, a few days after our talk with the children that I was extremely frustrated. Everyone was taking all this in stride like Horado and I had shared that we met in a class at the university, or that I had a new recipe for pozole I was going to try. That is when I realized, they were just what I knew they were, children. They processed what their experience and maturity level allowed. Things hadn't changed for them because this was still outside of their comprehension.

"Any new projects you are working on at school?" I asked Adelita that night at dinner.

"Nothing yet," she said between bites of her Cochinita pibil. This slow-cooked pork dish was Horado's favorite. Of course, I cooked it in a crockpot, not buried in the backyard wrapped in banana leaves as my grandmother had taught me.

"But you turned in your research project on your chocolate discovery?" I asked.

"Not yet," she said. "I turn it in at the end of the week, but it's done."

"Paco, how are things with you?" I asked, switching focus. "Any new challenges at school," I asked. I hoped he would have a little more information about some fight he averted recently, but hadn't wanted to elaborate.

"Meet any new girls?" Horado asked with a smile.

"No problems, no girls, just taking life as it unfurls," he said while chewing his food.

I thought I saw a flash of something in his eyes that quickly disappeared. Maybe it was my imagination. I will need to stay more focused on him. I had noticed that as things get so busy in my life, with Horado's travel, and Adelita's constant curiosity, it was easy to set Paco on the *everything is okay there* shelf.

"Don't talk with food in your mouth," I said feeling frustrated again and then embarrassed that I was frustrated. I should be grateful life was going well for them. I worked my zygomaticus major muscle to create an authentic smile. As I did, I thought about this tiny little muscle and one of its other functions, that of facilitating speech. I had come across the many powerful functions of this tiny muscle in a prerequisite biology class for my chemistry major. Just a seemingly insignificant muscle that didn't control a limb or critical body function, but that could change one's mood, or communicate to the mind, or to another person, powerful messages. I was deeply grateful at that moment for small and tiny things, like a bar of chocolate, or a facial muscle, that could change the world. Nothing brought more peace to my world than talking with my family.

"Any questions about what your Papá and I shared with you about our family?" I finally asked.

"Why did you give me my second name Naylay?" Adelita asked.

"Do you remember what it means?" I asked.

"It means girl with perception, right" Adelita said.

"Excelente, yes," I said. "Actually, your grandmother gave you that name when you were five years old. I don't think you would remember, but that was when your Abulela's brother died. He had supported her in Mexico and even paid for her move to the States because your Abuelo, my Papá, had died so many years before. We had not explained this to you since he had never left Mexico and you didn't know him. When we got to Abuela's house, you stopped in the doorway, and then ran to her and gave her a strong hug. You told her you were sad and sorry for her. Abuela had assumed we had told you about her brother's death. When I explained you had no idea what had happened, she gave you your second name."

"Your right, Mamá," Adelita said, "I don't remember that. I think I have always known that Abuela has had a lot of sadness in her life. I wish I could have known my Abuelo."

"And a lot of joy and comfort," Horado said, chewing on his food.

"Don't talk with food in your mouth, Horado," I said. He turned to Paco and smiled. I saw Paco smile back. "How am I ever going to teach your son table manners, when you are as bad as him?" I added.

Paco swallowed his bite of food and asked, "Is there a story behind my second name, my claim to fame?"

"Your Abuela named you too," Horado said. "The day you volunteered to walk Adelita to school on her first day. Your Mamá was going to drive her, but you said you would walk with her. That was being a good big brother. But when you two were walking by Abuela's house, she started to go leave the house to greet you both and she stopped when she heard you tell one of your friends to stop pestering Adelita or you would make sure he would arrive at school with a black eye. That was being a guardian."

"I remember that day, nothing much to say," Paco said. "He was trying to scare Adelita about her first day at school. He was being cruel."

"I do remember that day," Adelita said. "Pedro was being a jerk and I knew it, but I will admit his stories were starting to really scare me." She smiled at Paco and he smiled back. She turned back to me and asked, "Our second names are supposed to be like a goal, right? They sound like names we already earned."

"Those were just small indicators, just a foto, not the movie," Horado said. Your aspirational name, someone's hope or desire for that achievement," he paused and looked at me, "is that a good way to say it in English?"

"Perfect," I said. "Your Abuela saw something in both of you and claimed the privilege of giving you those names."

"Abuela's are always the ones who do the second name?" Adelita asked.

"No," I said. "It is traditionally the parents, but back in Mexico, it could be the priest, or a teacher, or the village together that decides on a name."

"What is your second name, Mamá?" Adelita asked. "I was thinking these second names were like secrets, but if the whole village knows, then what are your names, you and Papá?"

"I didn't get my second, or third name when I was young," Horado said. I knew he was trying to direct the conversation away from me.

"You didn't?" Adelita asked in surprise. "Why not?"

"I didn't grow up in a family with those customs and in a city that had forgotten the ancient ways. My names were given to me some time after I met your Mamá."

"Well, I think that is maybe even better because there would be less guessing," Adelita said. "You deserve a second name like Paco and me. The tradition is dumb if it can only happen when you are little."

"Don't make a decision on traditions when you have only now been introduced to them," I said. "Your Papá has second and third names. He just got them later in life. Remember though, sometimes things can only happen at one point in time and once past, that is the end to it. Your Papá was very good at fútbol when he was young. He could have played on the university team but decided instead to date me. He is now too old to play fútbol at that level. Time passed; door closed. In other situations, time, or age, don't matter."

"Your mother is right," Horado said. "I was very good at fútbol and actually I could probably still play at that level, but for sake of her example, I will pretend I'm too old. What would you say if I told you my second name is Messi?"

"Like the fútbol player?" Adelita asked.

"The only pretending you will do is thinking you are still twenty years old," I said. "I think I could agree with a second name messy, m-e-s-s-y. It would fit how you handle your dirty clothes."

"You gave up fútbol for Mamá?" Adelita asked. "That is so romantic."

"It wasn't fútbol or me," I clarified. "He just didn't have time for his heavy load of university classes and dating me. He could have done all three, classes, dating, and fútbol, but he wouldn't have done well at any of them. He was very good at dating me."

"So, your second name, Mamá?" Paco asked. "Is there a saga?"

"That is a story for another day," I said. "We have dishes to do, and you have homework to finish." I found it interesting that the children had completely forgotten to push Horado for his names and instead began to press me again.

"You can tell us while we do the dishes," Adelita said. "And my homework is just my report and that is already done."

"I'm done, no homework until the next sun," Paco said.

I was trapped. I looked at Horado who just shrugged his shoulders at me. Then he sat up straighter in his chair and said, "Like your Mamá said, that is a story for another day."

"It's okay if you don't want to share it," Adelita said.

The way she said those words hit me. It was like she knew she was still a little girl and somethings are just not shared with little girls. She was not a little girl and I knew I had to get over my silly annoyance, or embarrassment, or whatever I felt about my second name. I took a deep breath and let it out.

"It's just that there is a story that goes with the name and it's something I kind of don't like to talk about, so I avoid it. But you deserve to know it. Just don't judge me too harshly." I looked at Horado with raised eyebrows.

"I will start this out and Mamá can fill in the blanks where she needs to," Horado said. "This is actually an awesome story, and epic tale of a great heroine, an evil witch, and a handsome prince who was mostly clueless, but he was handsome, did I mention that?"

"Just get to the story, Horado," I said chuckling, more nervous than I wanted to be.

"Your Mamá did not receive her second name when she was a young girl, like you Adelita," Horado began. "She had to wait until later, like me. She was at the National Autonomous

University of Mexico, in Mexico City. This university is one of the most prestigious in the world, also the biggest in Latin America, on one of the biggest campuses in the world, in one of the biggest, if not the biggest city in the world."

"We got the picture Horado," I said. "Big."

"Abuela had sacrificed a lot to help pay for her daughter to attend the university," Horado continued. "Your Mamá is very smart, but this university is very demanding. She worked very hard and did well her first year. I don't think she even noticed that there were men in her classes. Shortly after classes started her second year, she was blown right out of her seat by a handsome prince in her Spanish literature class. Neither she nor the prince wanted to be in the class, but it was required. It became their favorite class, the one they looked forward to every week, because the other person was going to be there. The handsome prince could slay dragons with one hand behind his back and with only a pocketknife as a weapon, but he was scared to death to talk to this beautiful heroine."

I was going to interrupt again to get Horado back on the actual story, but I saw how much Adelita was enjoying this ridiculous version, so I kept quiet. I did roll my eyes at Horado, hoping he would take the hint. He was oblivious.

"The beautiful heroine princess actually talked to him first," Horado continued. "They became friends, then more than friends. They started dating. What the beautiful princess did not know was the handsome prince was being pursued by half of the female population in the university. It was his burden to carry, and he did so with apparent ease. By this point, however, he only had eyes for the beautiful princess in his Spanish Literature class. Certainly, his Dulcinea. But Dulcinea did not know that her handsome prince had recently dated another royal, at least in that other young lady's eyes she was. We will call her Lady K'abel. She was very jealous of Dulcinea and wanted the handsome prince back. The prince had no interest in returning. His heart was now fully given to Dulcinea."

"You know, Dulcinea was the imagination of an old Don Quixote with dementia," I finally interjected. "It was just me. A young and naïve student from a small town in Southern Mexico. I knew your Papá had dated before me, but as I began to fall in love with him, I forgot that there was any other history than the one we were making. I feel bad for Lady K'abel. She may have been mentally making the same history with herself in the lead role."

"That does not take away how wrong Lady K'abel was in what she did," Horado said, retaking the lead in this story telling. "She devised an evil plan to get Dulcinea kicked out of the university. She told a professor that she had seen Dulcinea cheat on several important exams. An inquiry was made, and it was decided that Dulcinea would have to retake those tests, but with different questions to see if she had cheated. This was a very hard time for your Mamá, I mean Dulcinea. She had worked extremely hard to get into this school and her family had sacrificed a lot to send her there. Now her integrity was unfairly attacked."

"Oh Mamá," Adelita said, "I am so sorry for you."

"This isn't the sad tale of Popocatépetl and Iztaccíhuatl," Horado answered. I wondered if Paco or Adelita even knew that story. I would have to tell it to them later.

Paco completed the rhyme with Iztaccíhuatl. "Get to the ending, don't dawdle."

"Word got around, thanks to Lady K'abel's efforts to spread rumors, that Dulcinea was going to have to retake those tests and was sure to fail," Horado continued. "This sort of thing just didn't happen in our day at the University. If people were caught cheating on a test, they lost the grade for that test. They weren't kicked out and they didn't have to retake the test. But Lady K'abel had pushed on this with university officials and wanted Dulcinea embarrassed and gone. Like your Mamá said earlier, time passed; door closed. Then Lady K'abel could have her handsome prince back. At least that was her plan, certainly not the plan of the handsome prince. It didn't work out that way. Dulcinea aced the tests. They were much harder than the original tests, with questions that weren't even in that section of reading. This not only closed the door on the threats of her expulsion but brought Dulcinea more notoriety as an excellent student. It also brought notoriety to Lady K'abel. Because of the big effort she put into this and her manipulation of professors and the university to do her dirty work, she was ostracized by the faculty and many students."

"She had a terrible last year and a half at the university," I said. "What should have been wonderful years, were lonely and sad. She did a wrong thing, but she shouldn't have had to pay such a terrible price. And I think she was very brave to stay at school through all that."

"Perhaps because of her loneliness, Lady K'abel got involved with a small group on campus that was involved with a Yucatan organization known as the Nobles. They claimed direct lineage to ancient Mayan nobility. This organization, at least in modern times, was, and is, no more than a group of people who dream up part truths to justify their personal greatness and who try to make money off of selling Mayan cultural heritage items for money."

"Just get to the embarrassing part of my name and we can close this story up and get on with our lives," I said. Horado was going to answer some unasked questions about the Nobles and I just didn't want to go there tonight, maybe never.

"Word of these things got back to your Mamá's village," Horado said. They were very proud of her and very unhappy with Lady K'abel who was from, as coincidence would have it, a neighboring village. Your Mamá was given the second name of Ajmac. It means the mind in a state of forgiveness and illumination."

"Ajmac, majac," Adelita exclaimed. "That is your second name. How cool is that. Why would you not want us to know that name."

"Because it is at the expense of another person," I said. "Lady K'abel also got her third name that year from her village. It was like an eternal prison sentence. Remember, the second name is aspirational, a goal for the future. The third name is usually given later in life as a gift for good things earned. She was given the name of *Tuus*. It means to tell a lie, to cheat, or deceive."

"That is sad," Adelita said. "Can't a person ever get a name changed?"

"I don't know," I admitted. 'Can a person forget their name,' I wondered to myself, 'and then create a new one because they can't find it?' "No matter" I answered for myself and to Adelita. "A name is a placeholder; it shouldn't be a judgment. Good or bad, our names, of course, are not the sum total of who we are. A bad person cannot hide behind a good name for long, but sadly a good person could be burdened with names that remind everyone of something bad."

"This lady is good then?" Adelita asked.

"I think most everybody has good in them," I said. "And everybody deserves the opportunity to let that part of them take the lead."

"When your Mamá heard about Lady K'abel's naming," Horado continued, "she arranged with the Canul family to give back some ancient property to Lady K'abel's family that has been held for many centuries and has been a point of contention since forever between the families. Unfortunately, the best your Mamá could get her family to agree to, was a long-term contract. Someday I will explain the details, but Lady K'abel's family, with good behavior, can buy it back in the future. That time is coming soon, I think."

"Is the lady doing okay now?" Adelita asked.

"She is married and they have at least one child," Horado said. "We hope the best for them. Now, you have the true story of the beautiful Spanish literature student and the handsome prince. Any questions?"

Paco and Adelita were quiet. "Did I mention the prince was very handsome?" Horado asked with a grin.

"I think that point was very well covered," I said. "Enough of my story, go make your own," I added, closing this topic. "I will do the dishes with the very handsome prince."

The next day I took my Mamá grocery shopping. I had already told her we had shared some of our family history and mission with the children. She had not been surprised at all that Adelita had found and figured out how to get into the Chocolate Room. "It is who she is, *mija*, my daughter," she had explained like I was the only child in this family event. "You could no sooner keep her from her discoveries, than you could keep me from a Vicente Fernandez concert."

"You have never been to a Vicente Fernandez concert," I said.

"That doesn't mean I didn't want to go," she said.

I didn't fight her logic. "Last night Paco and Adelita asked me about my second name," I told her as we unpacked groceries in Mamá's kitchen. "It went pretty good, I suppose. They didn't ask any hard questions about the Nobles. Adelita feels sorry for K'abel Xiu. And she wishes she could have known her Abuelo. My few memories of him only lead to more questions, so I stayed away from that topic."

"The Nobles and your Papá," Mamá said thoughtfully. "Two important topics that have been buried for a long time. I would like to keep it that way."

"Why Mamá?" I asked. "He is my Papá. Don't I have a right to know more about him?"

"You have the right to love him for who he was," Mamá said. "He was a very good person and loved you very much."

"It is hard to love one foto, five or six memories, and a mountain of mysteries," I said. "If that is all there will be, I will live with it, but his legacy will die with you."

"And that is a burden I will carry, for the sake of the safety of many, including you and your family," Mamá said, not realizing she had said so much.

"Now I really need to know about Papá," I said. "The safety of my family?"

"Oh, hija, let it be," Mamá said.

"Do you truly believe we will be safer being left in ignorance about whatever it is you are hiding?" I asked.

"I was sure," Mamá said. "The kidnapping of Horado by that *mequetrefe* Diacono has caused me to wonder."

"Good-for-nothing?" I asked. "Do you know Gerardo Diacono?"

"I know his family," Mamá said. "They are *alborotadores*, troublemakers."

I had noticed this before. When my Mamá was deeply troubled about something, she struggled with her English. Her mind could only speak in her native tongue. I switched to speaking Spanish. "The Diacono family has caused you trouble in the past?"

"They were partly responsible for the death of your Papá," she said.

"How did it happen?" I asked, hoping.

"He was on a delivery, of chocolate," she started. "His last of the year, even though it was only October. He was going to be home for many weeks. I was pregnant, maybe six or eight weeks along. He was going to help me through the holidays."

I already know more now about my Papá than I had known my whole life previously. Mamá had another child? I had so many questions, but I was afraid to break the spell. She was finally sharing. I held my breath, hoping she wasn't finished with her thoughts.

After what seemed like several minutes, she continued. "His chocolate delivery was in Mexico City, the Distrito Federal, to Alfonso Corona del Rosal, the Mayor. Tio Ignacio had foreseen something happening in the very near future. What did happen was the 1968 student massacre in Tlatelolco Plaza, the follow-on blatant security at the Olympic Games ten days later and how that impacted the lack of security in the 1972 Olympic Games in Germany and the terrorist attacks that would happen there. We didn't know all this at the time, of course, but we did know this was an important delivery that could make a difference with important events in the future, in Mexico and the world."

"I remember Papá saying he would bring me back something from Mexico City," I said, remembering his promise for the first time since he had said it. "I had no idea his absences were for chocolate deliveries."

"There were threats on his life," Mamá said, seeming not to hear my words. "But it was important that he make this delivery. Important decisions were going to be made and they had to be best decisions. The Nobles. They didn't know, didn't care, about our deliveries. They wanted the Chocolate funds. They wanted the treasure of Lake Izabal. Their black hearts were focused on greed, and they were going to get it no matter the cost. Their connection into our operations was Claudio Diacono. He is a great uncle of Gerardo, your present nemesis."

For fear of verbally interrupting again, I reached out and took Mamá's hand and softly held it. She smiled at me, but her eyes were far away. She looked much older than her 77 years.

"They knew Babajide's schedule and where he was going to stay," Mamá continued.

"Babajide?" I asked, not sure who she was talking about.

"Your Papá," Mamá said. "It was his second name. It is what I called him privately. It means 'Father is coming home.'"

"How beautiful," I said tearing up.

"We had hoped it would be prophetic," Mamá said. "He never made the delivery. Some ladrones the Nobles hired kidnapped Baba and told me I had 72 hours to deliver the funds to them, in cash. I got all the cash I could withdraw quickly, over $500,000 dollars, nearly a third of the fund in those days. Before I got to Mexico City, Baba and his kidnappers were killed as part of a Federal Police raid the night after the Tlatelolco Plaza killings. Neighbors had reported suspicious people in a motel room in Ecatepec. Some of their comings and goings seemed to be linked to radical student activities."

"That is terrible," I said. "I love that I am from Mexico, but there are times when we really get things wrong."

"That happens everywhere, hija," Mamá said. "It's humans that make bad decisions and that mortal frailty is not limited to any one country. In fact, there is no country immune from this nearly curable disease. That night has driven my passion for our mission ever since."

"How does that terrible night affect the safety of others that you would keep this a secret for so many years?" I asked.

"The Nobles felt threatened, so they threatened me and our family," Mamá said.

"I don't understand," I said. "Why did they feel threatened?"

"Communications with key members of the Nobles was found with the kidnappers and Baba," she explained. "Some of those letters gave information on your Papá's travel to deliver to the Mayor. It did not say what was to be delivered. Names incriminating some of the Nobles was also part of that, along with the kidnapping plans that did not mention who was the target, and finally, a description of me and that I would be bringing the money. None of it made sense without the context. The fear was the Federal Police, with their focus on the student unrest, would place all this in that context and an all-out manhunt would happen, leading directly to them."

"And to you." I added.

"That is what the Nobles used as leverage," Mamá said. "They sent Claudio Diacono to meet me. I knew he wanted the money, but that he felt very bad about the death of Baba. I don't think he wanted Baba dead. He, or rather the Nobles that were manipulating him, wanted the money. Anyway, he told me that the investigation could be closed for $50,000 and that I was to keep this entire incident to myself for the rest of my life. If I did not the Federal Police would receive incriminating evidence against me and our operations. If the police did not act, then the Nobles themselves would target me and my family, including you, who Diacono mentioned by name. I was forced to hand over $50,000, despite having just heard of my husband's death. I have no idea if that money actually went to pay off investigators, or lined the pockets of the Nobles, or Diacono made it up and it all went to him. No matter, it was disgusting money and I had a hand in it. Perhaps shame, along with fear, has kept me from telling this story all these years."

"I would have done the same to protect my children," I said, wondering what I would have been able to actually do in that situation. I think I would have just crumbled and quit. "So why tell me now?"

"There was never an actual agreement," Mamá said, "but it was understood that they would also back off and not bother us, as long as I kept my part of the bargain. You see, I also could have gone to the police and incriminated the specific Nobles, and Claudio Diacono who had much more information on them than I did. They also knew I had the funds to make it happen. They didn't know I would never use our family fund for such dirty work, but I didn't have to explain that. It was best to keep them wondering."

"So, the recent kidnapping attempt of Horado broke that deal?" I asked.

"That was a deal brokered with a past generation," Mamá said. "I doubt they think of this as breaking a deal. Even if they are aware of it, the statute of limitations has expired as their greed has grown. It is best that you know the history in order to make better decisions to keep your family safe."

"You could have shared this with me long ago," I said. "I can keep a secret and it would have helped me understand our family threats more clearly." I fought to control my emotions as I added, "And I would have known all these years that my Papá loved me and wanted to be with us."

"I thought it best to let you make your own assumptions in order to not burden you with extra worries," Mamá said. "I might have been wrong, but I don't know. I will let you judge me as you think through all this new information. Would you have had Paco and Adelita, knowing they were being watched and were threatened? Would you have continued with our family mission? I know you struggle with anxieties about this blessing that our family carries and sometimes you see it as a curse, or at least a heavy burden."

"I am carrying this, blessing, with energy and enthusiasm, Mamá. I see the good it does, and I am honored to carry on our legacy."

"And you worry about passing on this legacy to your children," Mamá said firmly. "It is not easy. It is not a game, or a silly justification for the comfort of always having the money you need to have a home, food to eat, and take care of the worldly needs of our family. All higher purposes require courage and sacrifice, and there will always be opposition. You are a wonderful daughter. You are an amazing mother and a near perfect wife and co-partner with Horado in keeping the family mission going. Our ancestors would be so proud of you."

I was not ready, or interested, in discussing my faults and few strengths. I asked, "You were expecting at the time of that event. I am an only child. What happened?"

"It was a great struggle to have you," Mamá said. "We tried to get pregnant for many years. I was 32 when you were born. The stress of that experience may have contributed to the miscarriage I had shortly after returning home from Mexico City. It was like an exclamation mark on my goal to protect you and keep this a secret. But I have you and you have grown up to be the most amazing hija, daughter, I could have ever imagined."

I realized that I couldn't judge. I had no idea what she had gone through. Mamá had carried our little family though the wilderness and not only survived but thrived. Our mission to her was not something she defined but something that defined her. In that moment I had the clearest and most intimate understanding of my Mamá that I had ever had. It was an intimacy that transcended our past relationship. It was as if I had just been born and was looking at my Mamá with the blurry eyes of a newborn, knowing with complete trust that she would love me and nurture me and protect me with every breath she took. I took my first breath that aligned with hers.

Chapter Nine

"I TURNED IN MY CHOCOLATE RESEARCH paper for Miss Topkin's class," Adelita said at dinner. "I shared that I found a stash of chocolate in the house. I didn't go into any details. I'm sure my grade will not be great compared to all the work I put into the research part, but better than trying to explain reality."

I left two candy bars on Adelita's and Paco's beds as a gift the day after their big discovery. I had hoped it would help Adelita feel better about turning in a report that lacked the more exciting truth. I was happy to hear her talk about it now in a positive way and showing she was already moving on.

A few days later, I also helped Paco and Adelita understand the AJMAC code. I drew the circle with the swirl in it on a piece of paper.

"This is the Mayan symbol like I explained to you earlier. Its name is Ajmac," I began.

"And it's your name too," Adelita added.

"That's right, and I suppose that is part of the reason this word means so much to me." I said. "It helps remind us of our family responsibility. It is a symbol on the Mayan calendar too. It helps people remember to always try to prevent mistakes. The center swirl represents the mind in contemplation, thinking; the three lines going in different directions represent wise decisions. It also means wisdom, sincere study, humility so a person can learn something new. This is where the chocolate comes in. Chocolate offers a person making a hard decision the space and energy to release old patterns, habits, or thoughts which no longer serve in order to make way for new ideas and opportunities to emerge."

"So, is that why you put the swirl and 'Itza majac day!' on all your notes? Adelita asked, "so I would make good decisions?"

"Well, it wouldn't help you much if you didn't know what it meant, right?" I said. "I put it there to remind me to make good decisions with you and to remind me to help you make good decisions. I put it on notes Adelita, Paco, because I love you. I wasn't actually trying to give you the secret password to the Chocolate Room. You figured it out because of your superb sense of observation." I said as I gave her a hug. She took a little nibble of her chocolate bar and smiled up at me. My heart melted faster than the chocolate in her mouth.

"Well, I think I got help from Tio Ignacio," Adelita said.

"Oh, and the word 'itza' was a little joke," I said, pretending not to hear her comment about Tio. I wasn't sure I wanted to get into that conversation. "It worked out to sound like 'it is a Majac day," but there is more to those words. Of course, majac was a silly replacement for 'magical, or great' or whatever meaning you wanted to put to it. As it is spelled it doesn't mean anything. "Itza, however, is Mayan for 'a wise person.' So, the statement really means, if you rearrange the letters of majac to ajmac, 'wise person, think; take a moment, and then make a good decision."

I asked again that evening at the dinner table, "So what do we do with all that chocolate?" and then turning to Paco, more seriously this time, "Except for the amount we might need to help us through our own challenges and problems—to help keep peace in our own hearts and in our own home." I said very slowly.

"Oh, I know!" Adelita shouted, too loud for the dinner table. "Can we share some with my friends who might need some help with their problems?!" She asked excitedly.

"This is the big secret. Is it really the chocolate that solves the problems?" Papá asked Paco and Adelita.

"Well, no, not really." Adelita said, trying hard to think of what Horado and I were really asking.

"Okay, here is the scoop, troop," Paco said to me. "Mamá uses the candy as a tool, but it isn't the solution to the actual problems, except maybe my hunger sometimes," he said with a grin glancing sideways at me. Paco grabbed the marking pen off the counter that I used to write Adelita's name on her lunch sack each day and drew two pictures on a napkin for me. It looked like this:

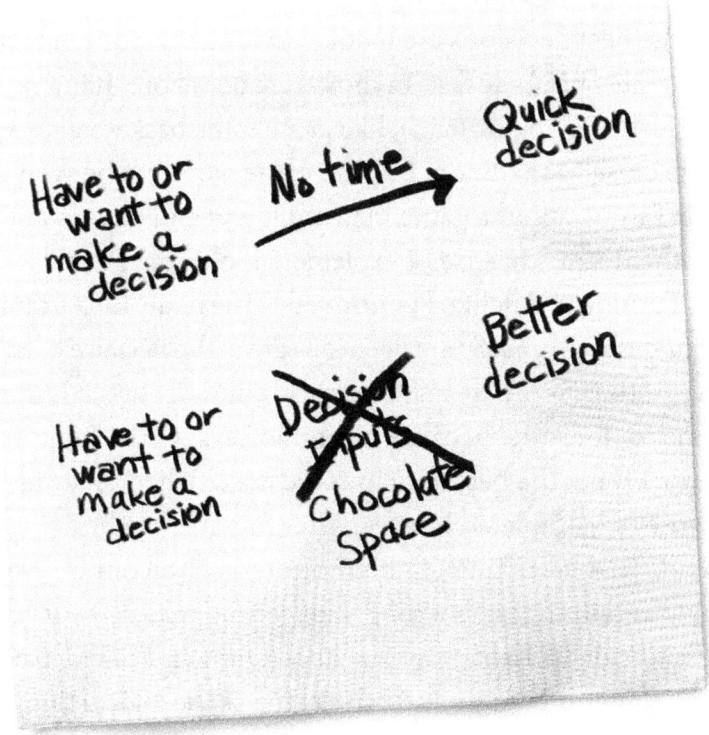

"You see Adelita," Paco continued, sounding like a substitute teacher; smart, but a little out of place, "Mamá is saying that interrupting a response with something that people like to do, like eating a piece of chocolate, gives them time to think things through and make a better decision."

I stared at Paco and not for the first time in the past few weeks I realized how grown up he was becoming. Then I grabbed his hand and asked with respect in my voice to hide the emotion, "Who are you and what have you done to my cute little boy?!"

Horado just chuckled.

"I don't just play basketball and belch," Paco said. "I know a few things I shouldn't squelch," he added with a smirk.

"We talked about this, well not the chocolate part, in Topple's class when I was in the sixth grade, and I just put two and two together," Paco said with an embarrassed smile.

"That is Miss Topkins, Paco," I reminded him, "but I am very impressed." Then to both of them, I continued, "Some people say the best decisions are made very quickly. Sometimes decisions must be made fast. In those rare occasions, it is a reaction, or a feeling in the stomach, like passing the basketball to a teammate close to the hoop. But the game wouldn't be won if you didn't think about a game plan and plays and how to adjust to another team's defense," I explained, looking at Paco.

Turning to Adelita, I continued, "The really important decisions deserve time. Some decisions are made because of habit or an emotion. Some are made because our heart says it is the right thing to do; some because our mind says it's the logical thing to do. I think the best decisions are made when the round-trip journey is completed between the stomach, the heart, and the mind. That takes time. Our emotions can tell our heart something and it might be wrong, like getting mad at your brother because you had a bad day at school. Our mind can help us with that. Sometimes our mind can say this is the logical thing to do, but it may not be the right thing to do, like telling Abuela she forgot the sugar in the cookies she spent all afternoon making for you. Our heart can help us with that. But it takes a little bit of time to make that round trip." I looked at Paco and Adelita to see if I was making any sense.

Adelita tried to look like she understood everything I had said, but her forehead was scrunched up. Paco was looking outside, lost in his thoughts, or maybe just bored and wanting to play basketball, since I had just mentioned it. I decided to press on before they completely lost interest. I opened my mouth to speak and was interrupted.

"Lots of information," Horado said. "Let's just leave all this with a wrap up and then go to the chocolate room for an official tour."

He looked at me and I smiled my approval. I didn't want to push any of this. "There will always be something unique and special about putting a piece of chocolate in our mouth. It does create a space, a brief moment or a longer time, to think before a decision, a reply or doing something important. For the ancient Maya, your ancestors, it was a way to break bad habits and find peace and consider new ways to see old things. We live in a crazy world today, full of surprises and hard decisions. Our family duty is to offer people a little chocolate space before they make their important decisions."

I was done, but then thought to add, "We believe that if we can help people make better decisions by helping them use their mind and their heart, we might just change the world."

After a tour of the chocolate room, Adelita went to the library to read and probably process all this. It was a lot to take in. After she started up the stairs I thought maybe this would be a good time to for some one-on-one time with her so I headed that direction too. Just before I topped the stairs, I heard Adelita talking. I stopped to listen.

"So the Canul family invented the 'chocolate space' for making good decisions and we have been saving the world by giving people chocolate to eat so they can think through their decisions?" She was saying.

I peeked to see her looking around the room like she was going to find someone hiding. She was definitely was alone. "Who are you?" Adelita asked.

"Tio Ignacio?" She asked as she turned her back to where I was mostly out of sight in the stairwell doorway. She was looking directly at Tio's painting.

"So, you are alive, inside the painting?" Adelita asked, sounding worried that she was maybe hearing things.

"But how, why, when did you get stuck in a picture?" Adelita asked with excitement laced with a little doubt and a little fear.

I remembered back to when Tio Ignacio began talking to me. It was hard to believe. So many doubts. So many fears. I was a college graduate. Adelita is twelve years old.

"So, you talk to my Mamá too? And my Papá?" Adelita added sounding like some things that hadn't made sense had just clicked into place.

I wished I could hear the other side of this conversation. I wanted to at least go into the room. I felt bad secretly listening in. I assumed Tio Ignacio was now explaining about the rules he operated by. "I can only talk to one person at a time and I don't choose the person," I could hear him telling me. What would this mean to the family? This means Horado is no longer hearing Tio Ignacio. Will he feel as left out as I have felt? Will Paco be jealous? Maybe mad?

"We can't all be in the same room?" Adelita asked.

"Why Tio, what is it I am supposed to hear?" Adelita asked now for sure sounding scared.

I think the first question I had asked Tio Ignacio was, 'Can you read the future, can you see outside of this room, what other magic can I do?'

"Right now, I want to understand what I am to do with this, gift," Adelita said.

I wanted to step into the library and answer all her questions. I realized I couldn't answer most of them. We have a painting hanging in our house that is of a dead uncle. That's not so odd, except he somehow knows the 600-year history of our family. He knows all our ancestors all the way back to our great, many great Abuela. He often knows who might need some chocolate, right now and in a month from now.

"Tio Ignacio, I am so happy to have a real conversation with you," Adelita said sounding very emotional. "I wish I could give you a big hug."

That did it. I entered the room to give Adelita that hug.

"Mamá, did you her?" Adelita asked.

"I heard you, Adelita," I said. "Did Tio Ignacio explain that he only talks to one person?"

"Yes. So only the person he talks to can hear him?" she asked.

"That's how it works," I said. "Well, I suppose I should say, that is the way I understand it. I never actually asked that question. I just accepted it. I asked some silly questions and usually I got only silence in reply. I think I have seen some slight facial changes, but I have never seen Tio move his lips and certainly not roll his eyes. That doesn't mean he wasn't doing so."

"Do I have to be in the library to talk with him?" Adelita asked.

"When you are talking out loud, it's best to be here in the room, mostly because others may think you have lost your mind," I explained. "You should be able to talk to him in your mind and he can reach you wherever you are."

"I am wondering," Adelita said hesitantly, "If he can only speak to one person and he is speaking to me, did I take him away from somebody else?"

"He began talking to me after I came home from the university. He stopped speaking to me when I married your Papá. We only communicated like you are doing now for ten months. He has been talking to your Papá for all of your lifetime and Paco's life too. He talked with your Abuela for about twenty years. I don't know before that."

"If Tio Ignacio was alive, I mean when he had a body," Adelita asked next. "I mean, he had a body a long time ago, but not that long ago really. Is he the only painting? Did anyone talk to the family before him? Another painting? Or is this just something we have now?"

"That is something to ask him," I said. "I knew some of the answer Adelita was searching for, but I didn't know if that was something I was free to share.

"I think I know enough for now," Adelita said. "I still have some reading to do before bed. Thanks, Mamá."

I had to smile as she went down to her room. She had just begun talking to a painting. The painting a person who lived a century ago. And she was worried about who she may have bumped from communicating with him. I had to admit, paintings had always communicated with me. I spoke back to them, in my mind, of course, and I usually didn't have to wait long for a reply. Some art offers a single conversation. Great art has many things to say, depending on the presence of the viewer. Like Horado said, "There are different ways art can talk back."

"Humans talk through art," my Mamá had told me when I was very young and had discovered an old painting that she was mailing to a museum somewhere else in Mexico. "And art talks through humans," she added while looking fondly at that painting of an ancestor; a lady with wild hair and a simple dress.

"They help us remember, they inspire, caution, entertain, visualize and explore. They offer us, truth, desire, discovery, values, principles, common identity, fears, beliefs, meaning, and more. Is it any wonder that painting has evolved like silica sand to transistor chips that transmit sound to our ears."

"Even more today," I thought, "from sand to silicon to transistors and the communication is two ways and ubiquitous. Brush strokes, paint, pigments, and form together transmit, but most people don't stop to listen. Maybe that is part of the problem. There is so much noise that counterfeits as communication, we miss the real thing."

I looked up at the painting of Tio Ignacio. He looked back with knowing eyes. He never blinked. "I seem to blink all the time, Tio," I said to him. "Is that why I had such a short time knowing you? I don't know what or who you are, but there are times when I wish I didn't have that short time with you and then have it take away so quickly and abruptly. Saying that out loud sounds so whiny. I am grateful for the experience. Really, I am."

I listened. I could hear my breathing. I could feel my heart. I continued to focus my eyes on the painting of Tio. He said nothing. I felt nothing new. I saw nothing change. I took a deep breath and let it out slowly. "Did I fall short?" I asked. "Did I do something wrong or not do something I should have done? My twelve-year-old is now your voice. I am thrilled for her. I am thrilled for the family and for our work. There is nothing else that is important to me. I will continue to grow up and work selflessly, so if you can hear me, I am sorry for all of my weary and dreary woes."

"Are you upstairs?" I heard Horado call.

"Yes," I answered. "Just talking with Tio Ignacio."

"Is he talking to you now?" Horado asked as he topped the stairs.

"No," I said, trying to smile. "He is talking to Adelita. I guess that means he is no longer talking with you."

"That's right," Horado said. "I offered my goodbyes the other day. I'm excited for Adelita. Wow, twelve-years-old and trusted with Tio Ignacio communications. That honors you as her Mamá. You have taught her well."

"You don't feel bad no longer talking with Tio?" I asked.

"I can still talk with him, like you were just doing," Horado said. "The answers will just come in a different way. He's not the Oracle at Delphi, nor a prophet, and certainly not God. I can go on without his direct presence in my life. He is useful to our work and as long as a member of the family is connected, we are good."

"You are right," I said. "We are good."

Chapter Ten

I HAD AN ODD SENSATION SENDING Paco and Adelita off to school the next day. I almost kept Adelita home. I felt like Pancho Villa's army was going to come over the hill at any moment and my children would get caught in the crossfire. I brushed off that foreboding feeling as my worries about sharing our mission with them took over my thoughts. And I was right. Paco and Adelita came home after a good day at school. Adelita had met a new boy, but he was going to be in the other sixth-grade class. Paco was outside in the front shooting hoops. Adelita was reading in the living room. I was enjoying working in our little garden in the back yard with Horado.

I had just finished transplanting our cilantro when Paco came running to the backyard. He didn't look scared, but he looked concerned.

"Papá," Paco said. "I was playing basketball in the front, and I noticed this car drive by a couple times. They slowed down by our house and then would speed up. They were an older couple, so I figured they were just lost. It wasn't like a gang car or anything. Then they both looked right at me and the lady in the passenger seat frowned at me like I was from a rival gang. It freaked me out. They just pulled into the driveway. Maybe it's nothing, but it didn't feel like nothing."

Horado went with Paco to see who it was. He was back in no time. "It's Hector and K'abel Xiu. This isn't a social call. They are sitting in the car discussing something. I thought about just talking to them while they were still in their car, but I'm not sure we would get a good answer. I asked Paco to wait until they come to the house, then go through front door and I am going to go in through the back door. I doubt this has anything to do with my attempted kidnapping, but you know how the Xiu's have maintained some links with the Nobles. Better we are safe than sorry, but we might still get some answers. Hopefully I am just overreacting."

"What do you want me to do?" I asked.

"Do you have your cell phone with you?" Horado asked.

"Yes," I confirmed. "It's in my back pocket. I reached back and touched it.

"I need you to listen to the conversation from the window. If it gets out of control, call 911. If they actually leave with me, which isn't going to happen, put Paco's bike behind their car. That will slow them down when they hit it. It won't stop them, but hopefully it will shake them up and will give us time to improvise our next move."

"Improvise?" I asked. "I don't like improvise. That is inviting trouble. They aren't actually going to hurt us. Hector wouldn't hurt a fly. I suppose K'abel is capable of doing some crazy things, but she is not that strong."

"Strong enough if she brought a gun," Horado said. "They aren't professional thugs and are probably improvising too, even if they think they have a plan. Don't get in the way if they do have a weapon. Promise?"

"Just get in there," I said, not wanting to waste any more time. I ran to the side window and listened. I heard Adelita calling for us.

"I'll get the door," Adelita called out. "I don't know where everyone else went," she exclaimed as she ran to the front door. "Probably one of Paco's friends and the emergency is some dumb basketball game and they need Paco, so they have enough players."

The doorbell rang again. "Someone is in a hurry," Adelita said. She didn't look through the peephole like I had taught her. She opened the door and the Xiu's were standing there.

"Oh hi," Adelita said. "Are you moving into our neighborhood?" She asked.

That was an odd thing to ask of total strangers, I thought.

"Is your mother and father home?" K'abel asked.

Adelita looked past them, looking for someone else. Maybe she saw Paco coming up the sidewalk to the house. "Just a minute, they are around somewhere," Adelita said. "Would you like to come in?"

"Yes, of course," K'abel said.

"I'm sorry, my name is Adelita," she said as they entered the house and walked into the living room like the owned the place. "May I ask your name? I'm sorry I didn't ask you earlier at school."

'Earlier?' I asked myself. She was so cute, trying to be polite, but was I missing something?'

"Xiu, Señor and Señora Xiu," K'abel said. She looked shorter and had filled out some since the last time I had seen her. She still had a pretty face, but she looked as stern as ever. Her ebony eyes and bob haircut and her stylish skirt and blouse made her look elegant if not older than she really was. I was surprised her husband Hector was about Paco's height. I hadn't realized Paco had grown so much this last year, or like K'abel, Hector had shrunk too. He was dressed like he was a rodeo empresario from Chihuahua. His kind face had not changed, and I took it as a good omen that he seemed relaxed.

"It is good to meet you again," Adelita said. "I will get my parents." She turned to walk toward the kitchen.

'Again?' I almost said outload. Maybe this wasn't going to go well.

"That won't be necessary, Adelita," K'abel Xiu said quietly. She grabbed Adelita's arm and started guiding her to the front door. She said something to Hector in Yucatec Maya that I couldn't hear. He went to the front door to open it.

"Lady K'abel," I heard Horado say as he entered the front room, "you are forgetting your manners."

The front door opened, and Paco stood there, looking bigger than I remembered him from two minutes ago. He was a full inch or two taller than Hector. He folded his arms and his eyes looked as tough as those of K'abel Xiu. She tightened her grip on Adelita's arm. I hadn't seen a weapon yet, but I got out my cell phone, ready to make a call.

Horado continued. "My daughter invited you into our home. Where are your manners? Were you going to leave before greeting us?"

"I would only come into a Canul home for business, never for pleasure," K'abel spat.

"And what is your business today?" Horado asked.

"You know our business," K'abel Xiu said, shaking Adelita's arm she had in her grip.

"We demand the money you have stolen from its rightful owners. The Nobles are losing patience."

So, they were here on behalf of the Nobles, I thought. Horado was right. I dialed 911, ready to push dial.

"The Nobles lost their patience over four-hundred years ago," Horado said. "Please let go of my daughter and leave our home."

"I will do what I please," K'abel Xiu said. "And it pleases me to leave. Come Jasaw."

"Lady K'abel," Horado called. She stopped and turned. "If you ever touch one of my children again, enter my home, or interfere in our work, you know what will happen. Consider yourself warned for the last time."

"The curse of the Red Queen be upon you and your family!" K'abel Xiu said. "Out of my way," she said to Paco. I flinched at K'abel's command, but Paco stood there like he was the door. He didn't move or look away.

"We will go peacefully," Hector Xiu said, speaking for the first time. "Lady Ajaw, the Red Queen, was not from Palenque like her husband and was very probably a Canul. I doubt she would curse her own family."

"May the Red Queen curse you then," she told Hector. I saw Horado nod, and Paco stepped away from the front door. His eyes were glued to K'abel Xiu until she was out the door, and it was closed.

"Will Mamá be safe out there alone with them?" Paco asked Horado.

"Oh, she can take care of herself. She and Lady K'abel go way back as you know," Horado said with a slight smile. "Lady K'abel Xiu will stay far away from your Mamá."

I smiled at Horado's estimation of my courage. I jogged to the front side of the house and watched the Xiu's drive away from our house before I went inside. "They are gone. Is everyone okay? Adelita? Let's send a box of our special chocolate to them. It looked like Hector could really use some." I was nervous and talking too much and I knew it but couldn't stop.

"Who's Hector again?" Adelita asked.

"Señor Xiu," I said. "K'abel called him Ajaw because that is his Mayan name. He probably didn't say much during the visit, did he?" I asked, not letting on I heard and saw the entire encounter.

"Enough to remove the curse of the Red Queen from our household," Horado said chuckling.

"We really should share with the Xiu's what Tio Ignacio told us about the Red Queen," I said. It had been a joke among those who knew Lady K'abel Xiu that she was no more related to the Red Queen than she was to Joan of Arch. Come to find out, in a conversation with Tio Ignacio, Horado had actually confirmed that K'abel really was related to the Red Queen. I guessed part of her claim of connection was more play acting then something she really believed. It would either create a bigger monster or calm her down when she knew the truth. I suspected the latter, possibly projecting my hopes for my own self-discoveries on her.

"It's her *conceived* idea of her connection with the queen that keeps her barely humble because of her doubt. To confirm her hope might lead to unintended consequences. Let it be," Horado said.

"Okay, you are both talking in riddles," Adelita said. What is going on? Who are they, who is the Red Queen, and what did they want?"

"Bad news comes in twos," Paco said plopping on the couch. "I'm glad they're gone, but for how long?"

"They won't bother us for a long time," I said, not sure I believed what I was saying. "Like any family history, there are things we left out when we explained the Canul family purpose and how we accomplish it.

"Nice Job, Paco," Horado said. "This could have been more complicated had you not noticed them and had that feeling something wasn't right. We had just enough time to get into place."

"So that's why you all disappeared?" Adelita asked.

"Paco saw them drive by a couple of times while he was shooting some baskets in the driveway earlier," Horado explained to

Adelita. "He had the presence of mind to come let me know when they started to pull into the driveway."

"Something didn't feel right, it was either flee or fight," Paco said.

"The Xiu family trace their lineage back to Mayan royalty," I said. "I think we touched on this briefly, but the Nobles are an old organization that claim royal heritage, but they are mostly a bunch of unethical businesspeople who sell ancient objects they have plundered from Mexico. They aren't quite grave robbers, but close to it," I added.

"K'abel is an on again off again member of the Nobles," Horado said. "She has tried to reform the group. And like we shared with you when we were explaining Mamá's name, Lady Xiu has a personal issue with both of us."

"K'abel Xiu feels like she is second place, and she also wants the money she says we stole from her," I added.

"You stole money from her?" Adelita asked.

"No, but one version of an ancient legend says the Canul family took a lot of money hundreds of years ago," Horado explained.

"If you do some research on the Internet," I added, "about an ancient Mayan treasure of gold buried in Lake Izabal, in Guatemala, you will discover that no one has ever found the treasure. They never will. The Canul family has had it for 600 years. At first it was kept hidden for fear the Conquistadores would take it back to Spain. Some say our ancestors started the Lake Izabal rumor to throw thieves off the trail in searching for it. The family has used the fund for chocolate production and delivery. It has lasted a long time because we have invested the money wisely and used the funds carefully."

"So, we are millionaires?" Adelita asked.

"Well, chocolate-millionaires," Horado said.

"And the Red Queen? She sounds mean." Paco asked.

"Lady Ix Tz'akbu Ajaw, the wife of Pakal that Paco is named after," Horado explained. "She lived around 650 AD, nearly 1,400 years ago. When archeologists discovered her tomb in an ancient city called Palenque, she had red dust all over her—something the Mayans used to preserve the bodies of royalty. They later identified it as cinnabar, the ground ore of mercury. Very toxic. They didn't know who she was at first, so they called her the Red Queen. Many stories grew up around her; curses, and crazy stories of her origin. Tio Ignacio told me she was from Vera Cruz, a part of Mexico north of the Yucatan where our ancestors come from."

"Lady Xiu is a sad person," I said. "She doubts she really is a descendent of the Red Queen and she wants so badly to be a warrior herself. She threatens us to get the riches she thinks we keep here in our house."

"In a way she is right," Horado said. "It was some of that money that paid for the chocolate equipment and it is what runs our chocolate operations. Those funds pay for our job and our living costs, shipping the chocolate. Our responsibility isn't just spending the money to deliver the chocolate, but also managing our money so it will always be available to support our family and our mission."

"How can you be sure they won't bother us again?" Adelita asked. "I thought they were going to kidnap me."

"I am so sorry you were put in that position. I promise you are safe and will not be bothered by them again. Hector lets his wife take the lead, but he is a good person and has his limits," I said. "He would have come up with a reason to not take you. I think he was counting on us to stop them."

"And the boy that was with them at school today?" Adelita asked.

"They were at your school?" I asked.

"They talked to me in the parking lot after school, like they were thinking about putting their son in my school."

"That is Bembe, their only child," I said.

"Bembe seems to be a good boy, quiet, obedient," Horado said. "Hopefully, he will take the best of both his parents and leave their less desirable traits behind."

"I thought he was cute," Adelita said before she could stop myself. She blushed as she tried to think of something else to say.

"Xiu and Canul, Montague and Capulet. He's the Romeo to your Juliet," Paco said.

"Impressive," I said to Paco. "I don't think I could have told you Romeo and Juliet's last names.

"Seventh grade English, something hard to extinguish," Paco said shrugging.

"I should have told you about them," Adelita said. "I saw them drive by earlier and just figured they were going to be our neighbors like they told me at school."

"Both of you make sure to keep us all informed about things that happen," I said. "We don't need to be paranoid, but when we all know what each one of us knows, we can make better decisions and stay safer."

"Plus, your mother is nosey," Horado said deadpan. "Best to keep her informed if Bembe asks you out Adelita. Better to hear it from you than Lady Xiu."

"Gross, Papá," Adelita said. "I'm in the sixth grade, not the twelfth grade."

"And you just keep thinking like that young lady," I added. We had a rule of no dating until sixteen years old. I knew there would be boys lining up on our doorstep before that.

"That would add an interesting dynamic to the neighborhood if the Xiu's actually did become neighbors," Horado said.

"That isn't going to happen," I said. "Lady K'abel Xiu, descendant of the throne of Queen Ix Tz'akbu Ajaw, the wife of Pakal, would not live in East LA."

"What's wrong with where we live?" Adelita asked.

"Nothing," Horado said. "Remember, we could afford to live just about anywhere, and we choose to live here. We love the diversity of cultures, the real people, good schools, and it is a perfect hub for our work."

"And they have the best tacos in the world outside of Mexico City," I added.

"Now you're talking," Paco said. "How about some taco stalking?"

"We just had dinner an hour ago," I reminded him.

"Exactly Mamá," Paco answered. "I've entered hunger trauma."

"Drop the drama and go get on your pajamas," I said.

Once the children were in their rooms doing some reading before bed, I cornered Horado. "Do you think the Xiu's will come back?"

"I have always had a hard time reading K'abel," Horado said. "I don't think her heart was really in it today. It was creepy when she grabbed Adelita's arm, but I could almost see her fighting herself when she did that. Did you hear the conversation?"

"I heard it and saw most of it," I said.

"It's easy for K'abel to act tough," Horado said. "That has been her persona ever since we've known her. It seemed more like play acting tonight."

"Do you think it will cause any emotional issues with Adelita?" I asked.

"I don't think so," Horado said. "Time will tell. I doubt Adelita and Bembe will ever feel comfortable being in the same room, though," he added.

"And the Nobles?" I asked. "Something is going on. There has always been a little saber rattling, but two direct attacks on our family in less than a month is something new. It's not natural for me to be on the defensive. Waiting, wondering. What can we do to figure out what is really going on? How can we be more proactive?"

"You want to launch a pre-emptive strike on the Nobles?" Horado asked, smiling.

"If that made sense, yes." I tried to smile too but couldn't. "Mama bear is bothered, and I need to hit somebody."

"I will stay out of your way," Horado said shielding his face with his hands.

"Wise choice," I said, starting to feel a little better. "Seriously, we need to figure out what is going on. Do you think you could reach out to Jorge Canul on the Council?"

"We could talk to him tomorrow," Horado said. "If he answers his phone."

"You talk to him," I suggested. "He doesn't take me very seriously."

"Don't let him get away with that," Horado said. "You want to be taken seriously; you take yourself seriously. Don't let his traditional Mexican machismo decide for you that you are a side show. You, my dear, are the main event."

"I'm not a circus act," I said.

"You're not a trained dog or pony," Horado said. "Jorge knows that. But are you the lion that he can manage with his whip, or are you the death-defying trapeze artist that flies through the air without a safety net? He would respect that as he got weak in the knees even trying to climb the ladder to get to you."

"Fine, as long as I don't have to wear a leotard," I said starting to feel a little empowerment.

"It would be okay if you saved the leotard for me," Horado said.

"*Tienes una mente retorcida*," I said. "A one-track mind." I socked him in the arm to add an exclamation point.

"Settled then," Horado said, not even noticing my pugilistic attempt to make a point. "It's midnight there. We can call in the morning. Now, what did you say about my one-track mind?"

Chapter Eleven

"**M**AMÁ, THIS IS STILL NUTS," Adelita said.

"Nuts go really well with chocolate," I answered with a smile.

"Some chocolates on their own taste nutty, delicious mouth putty." Paco laughed out loud.

Adelita ignored our comments and continued. "Tio Ignacio told me last night he was a university professor in Mexico before he, before he became a painting," Adelita said. "Hmm, it doesn't feel right to say, 'before he died,' because I can still talk to him."

"Did he tell you about how he became the most popular teacher at his school?" I asked.

"No," she said. "He seems to be a very humble person."

"Ignacio was also a very demanding teacher, and also very popular at his school. He was a nice man and a very good teacher, but he also handed out chocolate on test days. He was a Canul, after all. The students always assumed that he was just taking pity on them for his very hard tests."

"I need to give that idea to Miss Topkins," Adelita said.

"I am not sure that would be a good idea. There are too many concerns about child obesity and good diets in grade school," I said. "All these highly processed candy bars packed with sugar have given chocolate a bad name. Although that brings me back to Tio Ignacio. When I came back from college and Tio Ignacio started talking to me, I asked him about his days in college. He told me about his practice of passing out a piece of chocolate with the test papers."

"Wait, Tio Ignacio, you're talking to our family…" Paco said, looking for a rhyming word.

"Caravaggio?" I said filling in the blank.

"What's a Caravaggio?" Adelita asked looking at me for help.

"Caravaggio was an Italian artist who painted realistic looking paintings many hundreds of years ago," I explained, stalling. "Paco, the painting of Tio Ignacio is more than a painting. He really, actually, talks to one person. He chooses that person. He is talking to Adelita now. Please don't feel bad. He used to talk to me, but shortly after we got married, he started talking to your Papá instead of me. I got over it. Maybe one day he will switch to you."

"A talking painting, that's entertaining," Paco said. "Adelita has always talked to it, so only fair he talks back a bit."

"Good attitude Paco," I said, starting to feel relieved. "Tio Ignacio tried to highlight the health benefits of chocolate, such as lowering blood pressure. They didn't know about anti-oxidants back in his day."

"You mean chocolate is actually good for you?" Adelita asked in disbelief.

"In moderation, chocolate is good for your heart, and fights some diseases. It also improves brain functions. That was Tio Ignacio's theory in his day, but which science has more recently supported as close to the truth. I pushed Tio for a better answer, knowing the health of chocolate was still hundreds of years from being proven true."

"Well, what was his reason then?" Adelita asked. Tio Ignacio is sounding even more mysterious." she decided.

"He told me that he tried an experiment in his first year of teaching that had to do with our family mission to create a chocolate space for better decisions. He told me he noticed that many students went through the tests too fast. Often times they got answers wrong just because they answered each question like a rapid-fire machine gun. He tried handing out test questions one at a time, but that was too complicated because he had to wait for everyone to complete a question before going on to the next. Remember, this was long before taking tests with the help of hand-held computers. He tried several other ideas. Then one day he came to class with a bag of chocolates. Just for fun he handed out the candy during the test, explaining it was his birthday. He knew our family had been using chocolate to help create a better environment to think, ponder, and make better decisions. His thought was that should work for test-taking too. He noticed there were less mistakes on that test. That started his practice of handing out chocolate during tests."

"I can see why he was popular, that's very irregular," Paco said.

"He explained to me that, "It isn't so much the chocolate, but the process of slowing down thinking to a manageable pace. I have never admitted that to another student or even any of the other teachers. They would think I am crazy. Oh, and by the way," he added, "my tests are harder than the other teachers' tests, but my students almost always rate a few percentage points higher in test scores. The school thinks it is my teaching ability. I think it was the chocolate.""

"I had just finished college and I thought about his theory and added to it. What he was doing was not only slowing down the students' thoughts just a little, but he was also treating his students like people, not test-taking-machines, like so many of the other teachers. Because of that his students seemed to learn more in his class—so actually he was wrong, he really was a better teacher than most."

"Of course, he gave away chocolate, who wouldn't like that?" Adelita asked.

"It wasn't the giving away of candy that made him popular," I said, "it was the reason behind why he gave away the chocolate. He saw his students as special, and his students felt that long after the chocolate taste was gone from their mouths."

"Creating this chocolate space is supposed to help people make better decisions and feel more like people?" Adelita asked.

"Actually, it works better helping people feel more like people and then giving them the time to make better decisions. But yeah, it sounds like a stretch when you first think about it, I know."

"Tio Ignacio's little experiment is part of our family history but let me share some things with you and then you can get on with your day." I looked at Paco and then at Adelita. I started with a question: "Do you know what the Cold War was?"

"Sure," Paco said. "It wasn't really a war—more like the threat of war, between the United States and the Soviet Union."

"That's right, and it pretty much involved most of the world in one way or another," I said. "Those were very busy years for our family. After the Second World War there were two great super-power countries—the United States and the Soviet Union. They both had enough nuclear bombs to blow up the whole world and they didn't like each other; in fact, they were hated ene-mies. They didn't trust each other either. It was a very tense time. When I was a little girl, we would practice nuclear attack drills by getting under our desks. It made us all nervous, but as students we thought it would help. As I got older, I realized getting under our desks wouldn't even protect us from a hard wind, let alone something that could flatten a whole city... Anyway, there are at least a couple times when a nuclear war almost started."

I could see Paco was getting interested, but now Adelita was fidgeting. "Are you doing okay Adelita? This is a pretty deep discussion for a sixth-grader, isn't it?"

"Are we almost done Mamá? I know this must be important, but I have homework." she answered in a roundabout way to my question. I could tell she didn't want to hurt my feelings.

"Let me tell you two quick stories—in fact each story is about a person with a daughter and a son, not a lot different than you two—and both stories really happened. Looking back at the Cold War, two dates are really important to remember: October 22, 1962 and September 26, 1983. On the first date, President John F. Kennedy took the United States to DEFCON-2. That is the Defense Condition..."

"The what?" Adelita asked.

"The orders the President gives to prepare the Army, Navy, and Air Force just before going to all-out war. All he had to do was say, "Go" and we would have attacked the Russians. The Russians had brought nuclear bombs to Cuba and we were very close to going to war over it. Instead of actually attacking, President Kennedy thought about it again and didn't attack. In the end war was averted. Like I mentioned, at that time he had a daughter, her name was Caroline, and a son, named John. Caroline had been given a special gift of chocolate for trying to memorize a poem. What isn't well-known, what Tio Ignacio shared with me was, he ate some of that chocolate while making his decision. I am sure he thought about his children too, and their future, when he was deciding what to do. It wasn't our chocolate. We didn't deliver it. It doesn't matter who delivers it, or even if it's chocolate that is eaten. But this story does teach the point that taking a moment more can really help make better decisions."

"The other date," I continued, "is connected with a Russian Lieutenant Colonel named Stanislav Petrov. It was late at night and he wasn't even supposed to be at work, but he was there to help someone else out. He was in charge of monitoring the satellite system that watched for an American missile attack on Russia. His orders were, if the system detects an attack, you are to push the red button that says 'START' to launch a counter-attack—that is, shoot missiles with atomic bombs at the U.S. The system, just past midnight when he was probably getting really tired, sounded the alarm and said five missiles were just shot at Russia. He could have pushed the attack button and killed thousands, maybe millions of Americans and probably start an all-out war. He only had a couple of minutes to decide and he didn't push the button. It ended up that no missiles from the Americans were launched and later the Russians found out that their satellite was getting a signal from the sun's reflection off of some high-altitude clouds.

"Now that is scary! It could have been hairy." said Paco really listening now.

"Colonel Petrov said he was ready to push the attack button but took a minute to think about the situation. I think he may have thought for just a second about his son Dmitri and his daughter Yelena. Your Abuela told me that he had just opened up a piece of chocolate his daughter Yelena had secreted into his lunch for a surprise. I don't know if that is true, or if it was chocolate Abuela had sent to all the missile crew families at Tio Ignacio's suggestion. Whatever the case, it helped him stop, look at what was going on, and listen to his heart and mind together."

Paco and Adelita were silent for a minute, and I let them ponder what I had just shared. Then I said, "Those are two stories where something terrible didn't happen because a single person took an extra minute to think. Now why don't you take care of your chores, and we can talk again tonight or tomorrow. I know I have already mentioned this, but let's not say anything about the chocolate room to anyone though, okay? Can you imagine how hard that would make it for us to do our job?"

"Sure Mamá," both Paco and Adelita said in unison. Paco was gone in just a couple minutes to run a three-mile workout, in his new tennis shoes. I'm so glad I found that new shoe store in our neighborhood. Adelita went up to the library, probably to think this whole thing through and maybe talk it over with Tio Ignacio I was guessing. I didn't want to intrude, but curiosity got the better of me. I took up my post on the stairs by the library door.

I heard Adelita ask Tio Ignacio, "So what do you think about all this? We have a chocolate factory under our house. Oh, you probably know that part because you are home every day while I am at school."

As I prepared myself for hearing a one-sided conversation, I heard Tio Ignacio ask, "So, what do *you* think? Is everyone in our family just totally crazy? Inheriting a duty to share chocolate with people. Some people inherit wealth, others a skill at music, or art, or science. Some inherit bad habits that their parents taught them."

"We are an awesome family," Adelita said. "But how can just the four of us save the world? There must be a million decisions made every second. Even with the giant chocolate room we can't make that much chocolate, and then how do we know who to send it to?" I was feeling overwhelmed instead of excited. "And it's not just that, but we have people trying to stop us too," she added, probably thinking of K'abel Xiu.

"I wish I could tell you the Xiu family is harmless," Tio Ignacio said. "They were once our greatest allies. The Canul Family own several cenotes—remember those deep pits with water in them where Cacao was originally grown?"

Adelita was silent, but I guessed she had nodded yes because Tio Ignacio continued, "One of those cenotes was originally owned by the Xiu family. When I was young, before I died and became this portrait, I managed the family money. The Xiu family was not as wise with their money and found themselves almost homeless. I bought their cenote for twice its value to try to help them out. Later, thanks mostly to your Mamá when she met Lady Xiu at the University, our family set up an agreement to sell it back to the Xiu family in thirty years at the same price or lose it forever. We would like to sell it back to them, but Lady Xiu has been difficult. She says we should give it to them and pay them a fee for "renting it" for the last century. She knows the thirty years is almost up. Hopefully, they can follow through on the original agreement."

"So that's the threat my Papa mentioned," Adelita said mostly to herself. "This whole chocolate thing is more complicated than I could have imagined, and I have a good imagination."

"And as for who and how to deliver your chocolate," Tio Ignacio continued, "focus on helping one person at a time. It will make a difference for that person and then you will help another person. You will never help everyone, but I know you Adelita, you will make a difference. Did I ever tell you about the time your ancestor gave a piece of chocolate to Benito Juarez, the President of Mexico, after our country was taken over by the French? He felt completely alone and without options. He went on to free Mexico and become a national hero."

"Thank you, Tio Ignacio," Adelita said.

It stayed quiet and I crept back down the stairs. What had just happened? I had heard both sides of the conversation. My Mamá had mentioned when Tio Ignacio had shifted from talking to her to talking with me that there were unique time when more than one person could hear Tio. Was this one of those times? Did Mamá listen in on some of my early conversations with Tio?

"Tio Ignacio," I began, "can you hear me; can you talk to me?" I listened. It was silent. "I assume you can hear me, even if you can't or won't reply to me. Thank you. It was great to hear your voice and it was wonderful to hear you talking to my little girl."

I didn't want to wait until the next time I could visit with Mamá. I called her on the phone.

"Hola hija," Mamá said. "Is there an emergency?"

"No," I said. "Do I have to have an emergency to call you?"

"You almost never call me," she replied. "I love that we can talk in person, and I know I'm not the best person to keep up a conversation on the phone. I get distracted too easily. What are you calling for?"

"I do have a reason," I admitted. "Sorry, I will call more just to talk, no reason other than I love you and want to hear your voice."

"Digame," Mamá said. "Tell me, what is on your mind?"

"After I started talking with Tio Ignacio and then Horado took over shortly after that, did you ever get to hear him also?"

"No," Mamá said. "I have heard of that happening, but those are only family folktales. Stories of the whole family being able to communicate with the painting, Tio Ignacio, or the artwork before him. I have never talked to anyone who that has happened to."

"You have now," I said. "It happened to me today. Adelita began a conversation with Tio Ignacio and all of the sudden I could hear his side of the conversation. I don't know if this is the way it is going to be from now on, or if that was a one-time thing, but it was awesome."

"Tio doesn't answer you when you talk to him directly?" Mamá asked.

"No, he doesn't," I admitted. "I don't hear Adelita through Tio either. I was near her, though, so I could hear both sides of the conversation that way."

"I would speak with Adelita," Mamá suggested. "Have her talk to Tio again and see what happens."

"I thought of that," I admitted, "but I was worried that maybe I was supposed to listen in confidentially, without Adelita knowing."

"Tio Ignacio is usually clear in his directions," Mamá said. "I think if he wanted to keep it confidential, he would have let you know. Go talk with Adelita."

"Okay Mamá," I said. "I will let you know how it goes."

"Adelita," I called to her room. "Can you come up to the library?"

Adelita met me there and I explained, "I overheard your conversation with Tio Ignacio. I actually heard Tio's voice."

"That is exciting, Mamá," Adelita said. "We can work as a team. This has been scary, being the only person in the world that can hear him."

"That is why I am explaining this," I said. "I tried to talk with him afterward and all I got was silence. I was wondering if you could talk with him, and I could see if I hear him."

"Tio," Adelita asked, "are you hearing Mamá?

Adelita listened and repeated the words as she heard them.

""Sometimes, when it relates directly to the Chocolate mission," Tio Ignacio says. Hopefully I will get it right. . "She can talk to me and I won't necessarily hear her. I know that sounds flojo, wishy washy, but I don't really know how it all works either.""

"I can't hear him now," I explained to Adelita. "That must have been some unique event. Ask him if he knows anything about a museum of paintings like himself."

"Tio, is there a museum of paintings like you?" Adelita asked.

She listened and nodded her head several times. Turning to me she said, "There is a museum. It is a by invitation only museum. He doesn't know exactly where it is, except it is in southern Mexico. That is where he will go to retire someday."

"That is for another day, then," I said. "You are Tio Ignacio's right-hand girl, Adelita. It was great to hear Tio's voice after all these years, but I can't think of anyone I would rather have as our connection to Tio, than you."

"I wish you could be on the calls with me," Adelita said.

"I'm just on the other side of those calls, hija," I said as I gave her a hug. I hugged my little girl and I hugged out the little girl in me that deep down wished I could be in her shoes for just a little while.

Chapter Twelve

A COUPLE OF DAYS LATER I found Adelita in the library looking at Tio Ignacio.

"Are you and Tio talking?" I asked. "I don't want to interrupt."

"No," Adelita said. "I could live up here if you would bring food up to me. I was studying Tio Ignacio's portrait, trying to understand how it worked."

"Tio Ignacio knows but he is going to let me try to explain it," I said. "Can I join in the conversation Adelita?"

"Sure Mamá, Tio Ignacio isn't very talkative today anyway."

"You know there were days when I was your age and I would talk to Tio Ignacio, long before I could hear him, and I couldn't get a word in. Mostly I would just listen."

"Listen to what, if you couldn't hear him and you weren't talking?" I asked.

"I listened to the silence. I listened to him listening to me. We had a listening conversation."

"That sounds boring," Adelita admitted.

"Do you ever listen to the wind, or the quiet when the snow is falling, or leaves falling from a tree, or the waves of the ocean?"

I asked. "It's like a song. If we get too busy, let all the noise of the world into our heads and heart, we won't hear the song."

"*H ti, T u belil*," Adelita repeated obviously focused on the new words.

"Is Tio Ignacio singing?" Mamá asked.

"I think so," I said. "It's not a regular song and I don't know the words. I was wondering if there aren't any words how you can sing a song. I was going to ask you and Tio started singing."

"That is one of his favorites," I said. "It is a song in Mayan that can be translated to the word 'Dawn,' like when the sun is first coming up. He told me this song is from a town close to where our family comes from. The town is Dzitbalché, in what is now the Mexican state of Campeche."

"What do the words to the song mean?" Adelita asked.

"'For the traveler, who is on the road,' the Mayan words are *H ti, T u belil*;" I began. "'If the sun should come here.' *Ua u aal kin Uay*. This is a song about all of us. We are travelers because we aren't frozen like a statue. We move, we breathe, and we make decisions. The song talks about the birds we see in the sky. Then it ends with the words, 'Only songs and play pass through their thoughts.' *Chen kay Chen Baxaal C u man T u tucuuloob*."

"It sounds pretty," Adelita said. "Especially when Tio Ignacio sings it."

"He is teaching you Adelita," I said. "He loves to teach by singing. The words are easier to remember when they are sung, but they mean much more than what we might first think."

"Like what?" Adelita asked.

"The traveler is us. The sun is coming up—it's a new day. But that could mean we have a new challenge to face, a new decision to make. So, what could the birds represent?" I asked.

"Things we see?" Adelita guessed.

"Yes, that's good," I said. "They could be distractions. They could be answers to our questions, they could be new discoveries we weren't even planning on finding. They are those inputs between stimulus and response that Paco drew for us, remember? The birds are in the chocolate space. And then the song ends with the words, 'Only songs and play pass through their thoughts.' So, the traveler, you and me, are trying to make decisions and the inputs we have to make those decisions fly through our minds like birds. The songs and the play of those  birds pass through our thoughts. The song is like the Ajmac swirl that is our family symbol. It kind of looks like this song to me. We travel on the road that goes around and around as we try to make good decisions. The swirl with the lines coming off of it could also be the sun, like the song's name suggests, the dawn of the decisions we have to make."

"And the swirl to me," Adelita added, "looks like a 'P' standing for paz, peace. Chocolate peace."

"Cool," I said. "I never thought of that. It does feel peaceful. The swirl is something I see in nature everywhere, and it always feels restful and harmonious. Kind of like the listening conversation I was talking about. Maybe that is why Tio Ignacio sang that song to you."

"Wait Mamá," Adelita said like she was listening to someone else. "Tio Ignacio just interrupted what you were saying." She listened again for a brief moment. "We have a chocolate emergency. There is a boy named Jaime that is only two blocks from here. He needs some chocolate right now! What do we do?"

"We get him some chocolate!" I said. I will get the chocolate. You go get your brother Paco."

A minute later I handed the chocolate to Paco who rode his bike to the address Tio Ignacio gave Adelita. It was only two blocks away. Paco knew the boy even though he was a year older. Paco was back in fifteen minutes.

"That was close, Jaime was almost comatose," Paco said. "He got mad and was going to do something bad."

"It wasn't chocolate that helped him make a decision?" Adelita asked.

"He was making a decision. He was going to run away, making a life revision that was headed for a collision," Paco explained. "The stress of his mess caused him to think less. He put his decision on pause, to consider the cause."

"And that's how it works?" Adelita asked. "Tio Ignacio tells us who needs the chocolate, and we deliver it?

"Sometimes we deliver," I said. "More often we mail it, sometimes to faraway places. Mostly I do the mailing and your father does the traveling, when personal deliveries are needed. Now that you and Paco are involved, we will ask for your help. A few times in our family history we delivered the chocolate to faraway places in person. It took many days, sometimes weeks to deliver the chocolate. Of course, hundreds of years ago, there wasn't a way to mail things, although Tio Ignacio did tell me how we used Pochteca, the long-distance traveling merchants in the Aztec Empire."

"What if I know someone who needs some chocolate space?" Adelita asked. Do I have to wait for Tio Ignacio to tell me to take some chocolate to them?"

"Oh, not at all," I said. "In fact, I would guess that more than half of our chocolate goes to people we have decided on our own to deliver our special chocolate to. Sometimes it is a rush job. Most of the time it is something we can send through the mail."

"Are you okay honey?" I asked, noticing Adelita was suddenly very quiet and looked pale. "All this talk about scary things and the surprise of the Chocolate Room. That is a lot to take in."

"Not to mention a painting that talks and sings," Adelita added. "And only to me. What if we can't get chocolate to people in time and they make a wrong decision." Adelita asked.

"We won't be able to help everybody, ever," I said. "But we can do what we can do. For example, what world leaders could use a little chocolate, and maybe what groups of people going through hard times would smile with a gift of chocolate? What do you think?" I asked encouragingly. "We have the capability to reach out to just about anyone. A local leader, or the head of a foreign government. Actually, I have been counting on your great imagination as much as your superb gift of observation, to help me do a better job at this."

"I still don't see how a chocolate bar is going to make a difference with some leader of a country. A simple candy bar is nothing compared to some really scary and serious problems."

"Adelita, you can't believe peace in your own heart is possible, and not believe in peace in the rest of the world…even when it seems nearly insurmountable to achieve."

"You're starting to sound like Papá," Adelita said.

"Well, that is how I see it. It just wouldn't be right to not do something—if we can. And just because we can't do it all perfectly, or that it seems small and maybe silly to some, doesn't mean we shouldn't do what we can. There are a lot of things we can do that will make a difference in our home and in the world. And before you bring it up later, some people are just bad and the best a chocolate bar would do for them is to help promote their tooth decay. We will send them chocolate anyway. It is up to them what they do with their chocolate space.

Thankfully, most people are basically good. They just need to think—you know complete the round trip between the stomach, the heart and the head. A chocolate bar break, the chocolate space, won't save the world by itself, but it might just plant a seed in somebody's thoughts that will lead to another thought and an action and then another thought that eventually could lead to making a huge difference."

"I also think," I added before stepping down from my soap-box, "if the chocolate came from an anonymous sixth grader, that might have more impact than anything else. Nations and leaders of nations have agendas. Most adults have a perspective or viewpoint. A sixth grader usually doesn't have an agenda that would create distrust. And sixth graders naturally treat people like people. Even hardened world leaders know that." I waited for a response.

"Okay Mamá," Adelita said. "But you haven't been to the sixth grade in a long time. Believe me, there are agendas and many minds are already made up."

"And we can help change that, one piece of chocolate at a time," I said.

"If you believe it, then I will help as best I can," Adelita said.

"Help make a difference!? Are you kidding me? We are pretty good at this already. Did you hear about the terrible war and violence in Nepal not long ago?" I asked.

"No," Adelita said.

"Exactly!" I said. "That was chocolate diplomacy at its best, thank you very much. On the brink of all out civil war and after 19 days of a country-wide general strike, the King reinstated Parliament. The Nepali Congress unanimously nominated President Koirala to head the new government. All their problems aren't solved, but all they needed was a little chocolate space to get this far. Lucky for chocolate diplomacy, the King has a sweet tooth," I shared with a knowing wink.

"So, what can I really do, Mamá?" Adelita asked, still not convinced of her value in this family business.

"The question is, what can we do together?" I asked. "Remember, this is a family responsibility."

"When you say it that way, it sounds even more fun. We would get to see Paco more—especially if he got to be in the

Chocolate Room…but you would have to keep an eye on him, or he will eat up everything we make."

A few days later I noticed Adelita was humming Tio Ignacio's song. She had just gotten home from school. It appeared to have been a good day. "I secretly left chocolate in the lockers of two girls that were mad at each other," Adelita announced. "At the end of the day I saw them walking home from school together. Chocolate in exchange for peace." She stopped suddenly and looked at me. "Chocolate4Peace," she said out loud.

"What do you think?" she asked with excitement in her voice.

"Chocolate for Peace…" I said out loud. "Oh, I get it! Chocolate for peace and Chocolate four Peace, us, the four Chocolate makers working for peace. Now that isn't a half bad pun. Papá will like that idea," I said.

"So, Chocolate4Peace we are!" Adelita exclaimed. "We can brand the chocolate with the swirl and put it in a bag or box with a note that is from Chocolate4Peace. But how can we afford all this extra stuff?"

"You don't have to worry about the costs," Papá explained, walking into the room. "Remember what I told you about the Canul money that has been invested by and in the Canul family for hundreds of years? We can afford it if we are wise."

"I don't think we can afford not to do this," I said. "This helps send our message and over time our chocolate will be trusted. Unlike ancient days, the chocolate is not trusted today. Leaders worry about health, potential poisoning, and who knows what, and it goes to the trash or to someone else, not the leader it was intended for. That simple change becomes the focus and the chocolate's job is to carry that message."

"I think we ought to have a website to give Chocolate4Peace a floodlight," Paco chimed in.

"Could we maintain our anonymity?" I asked. "I mean, could we have a website that wouldn't lead people to our front door?"

"No big deal, that's easy to conceal," Paco said.

"It is sort of sad that we haven't moved into the new century," I admitted, thinking about the possibilities. "We wouldn't want people to tell us their problems, necessarily, but we could send them the chocolate, so they could reach out to people they know that are struggling with a decision. It would be quite a message if a whole group of sixth graders sent the mayor chocolates to help him with a specific decision."

"It would also give more people my age a way to get involved," Adelita added. "They would have to know more and then do something. Observe, right Mamá? See and do."

"Your Papá and I will talk about this," I said, glancing over to Horado. "I am still not convinced that we could keep ourselves distanced from people who would want to get into our business and make us the center of attention. We are behind the scenes, nearly anonymous supporters. That would take the humility out of what we do."

"More people to touch, fear of tech's a crutch," Paco said.

"You might be right, Paco," I admitted, "but I was taught to error on the side of caution with our mission. We could touch a lot of people for a short time and then the unintended consequences come along and shut down the whole mission and all the people we could have touched in the future would lose out."

"I see what you mean, have respect for the unseen," Paco said.

"What we don't know that we don't know is where the biggest dangers lie in wait to cause the train wrecks. We have been doing this for six-hundred years. I want to use technology, but I want to do so in a way that first does not cause big problems."

My thoughts were going a hundred miles an hour. I used talking to Horado as my excuse for setting this idea on a shelf because I didn't want the children to get too excited or too far ahead of ourselves. In reality we would probably need to run this by the Council and they are more old fashioned than my most Luddite days. We had the right to disregard the Council, but that caused other complications. On the other hand, I can't believe we had never even thought of this idea before, even in conversation.

Chapter Thirteen

"MAMÁ, DO YOU TRUST ME?" I asked.

"Mi hija, what a silly question," she replied. We had just left the doctor's office. My Mamá was in good health, but the doctor had given her some strict dietary warnings that I was certain she would not follow. "Why do you ask such a question?"

"And what about Tio Ignacio," I added. "Do you think he trusts me?"

"I don't think that old painting has the ability for trust or distrust," Mamá said. "As for me, of course I trust you. Your character is beyond reproach and you are always truthful."

"That is being trustworthy," I said. "They are not the same. You are describing me. Being trusted comes from you and your decision about me."

"Why the questions and the fist fight with words?" Mamá asked again.

"We just listened to your doctor explain your health," I began. "We trusted him not just because he is reliable, but we took him at his word, with certainty and well-grounded hope. We didn't question his assessment of your health. That seems risky. He is human and imperfect."

"What does that have to do with you? Mamá asked. "I trust you more than my doctor, but I wouldn't want you operating on me."

"You trust me, I suppose, because I know better than to operate on you," I said with a laugh I didn't feel. "I was thinking about trust and how our family business operates. How Tio Ignacio operates."

"It is amazing that our family is trusted with such an important mission," Mamá said.

"Trusted with the mission and with the funds to accomplish the mission," I added. "We could live like kings for many generations with that money, and not ever lift a finger to help people make better decisions."

"Then answer the question yourself, hija," Mamá said. "Do you trust yourself, and why or why not?"

"Great question," I said. "Isn't that part of what we do? We challenge people with chocolate space, that time in between stimulus and response where we hope the decisionmaker can overcome emotion, intuition, habit, ego, and expectation, so they can harness better understanding, principles and wisdom for those breakthrough decisions."

"Ay, hija, what are your talking about?" Mamá asked, goading me.

"I want to say I trust myself, but I know that desire, that decision, is packed full of emotion, ego, and expectation," I said. "I am looking for some external markers. I think all I can decide about myself is whether I am trustworthy."

"Deep doubts, deep wisdom; small doubts, small wisdom, my Abuelo use to say," Mamá said as she considered my explanation. "Those are the considerations of a person the world should trust. An awareness of those shallower motivations highlights someone others would trust. But am I hearing something else in you words? Perhaps the first question is, what are you afraid of?"

"Afraid of?" I asked.

"Are you afraid of failing?" Mamá asked. "Is there another fear? I think people struggle with trust, of themselves or with others, usually have bigger issues behind their eyes. The irrational fear of being too happy might lead to sadness, hurt, or apathy. Fear of peace and satisfaction because it could all be taken away. Fear of not being good enough to warrant your desires or goals. Fear because you know your imperfections and past failures, so how can you ever measure up. Fear because comparing lots has you in a constant downward spiral. Many fears are possible mi hija."

"I don't think I have an irrational fear," I said. "I do think it is usually the people with big blind spots that are overconfident, over certain about themselves, and that wise people are not as quick to assign themselves with such certitudes."

"Wisdom is not incompatible with confidence and courage," Mamá warned, shaking her finger at me. "You are courageous, hija. Is that why you have doubts about self-trust?"

"Why do you think Tio Ignacio only spoke to me when I was older, and only for a few months?" I asked.

"Is that where these doubts are coming from?" Mamá asked. "Like I said, I don't think that painting can trust or distrust."

"Yet we trust him," I countered. "Horado puts his life on the line at the direction of that painting. Adelita is 12 years old, and she is the sole hearer and voice of that painting. I have to trust him to not lead my daughter astray or into danger. Adelita trusts him. You trust him."

"You are right," Mamá said. "I trusted him as a 12-year-old, just as Adelita and I never lost that young girl acceptance that it was what our family did. We trusted Tio Ignacio, and Tia Izel before him."

"Tia Izel?" I asked.

"That was the painting before Tio Ignacio," Mamá explained. "My Mamá told me about her. She was retired during my Mamá's time of hearing the painting. She appreciated Tio Ignacio's singing and straightforwardness, but she told me she missed Tia's enthusiasm and her humor."

"You never mentioned there was a painting before Tio Ignacio," I said.

"You never asked about it before," Mamá countered. "I've never thought about it this way before, but I see that our family mission is not only to create chocolate space for people making decisions. Our mission demands that we be trustworthy and trusted. You have taught me this, my daughter. I have also come to understand that Tio Ignacio, if he trusts, must trust most those who know of him, but do not hear him. So, to answer you first questions, yes, I trust you and yes, Tio Ignacio trusts you."

"I believe you, Mamá," I said. Maybe my problem is, I have been hearing the silence of external votes of trust as a sign of distrust, if that even makes sense."

"Distrust is not the absence of trusting," Mamá said. "That is less trust all the way to untrusting. I don't know what the dictionaries say, but the way I see it, trust is a person's confidence in the positive. Distrust is confidence in the negative. Both are just looking for certainty. That's what we humans do; we look for certainty."

"Have you always been this wise, Mamá?" I asked.

"Have I always been this old?" Mamá asked back.

"Well, thank you for your aged wisdom," I said. "Oh my, I didn't realize how long we have been talking. Could I swing by my house before I take you home? I need to make sure Adelita and Paco are home from school and that they know I am home. I didn't leave a note."

"Where is Horado?" Mamá asked.

"He traveled to Mexico to meet with the Council," I said. "I am not happy about it, but it couldn't be avoided. We are having issues with the cacao pod shipping. It's new for them. They always did the manufacturing, not shipping of raw materials. Remember, it was just a few weeks ago that he went to meet with them and was kidnapped. I'm stressed. Stressed for his safety. I'm stressed for our family's safety. I'm stressed I'm not doing things right. Paco and Adelita seem way ahead of me, but I'm the mom and need to watch out for the things they may not be prepared for."

"All is well, hija," Mamá said rubbing my shoulder as I drove us to my house. I was grateful the doctor's office was only twenty minutes away. "Your children are good and are learning to live by principles. There will be surprises, but together our family will find a way forward."

I knew Mamá was right. My anxiety went down, and then started to climb when I approached our house. There was a bicycle parked on our porch that I didn't recognize. Probably a friend of Paco.

We entered the house and there was a boy coming down the stairs, but not with Paco.

"Adelita," Abuela asked. "Who is your friend? He looks familiar."

"Hi Mamá, Hi Abuela," Adelita said. "You are home early. This is Bembe Xiu."

"Yes, of course," Abuela said. "You are the son of Hector and K'abel. It is good the Xiu and Canul family are together again."

"Not so fast," I said to my Mamá. Turning to Adelita I asked, "What is going on Adelita? I'm okay with you being friends with Bembe, but not alone in the house with him. And you look really stressed. Is everything okay?"

"It's not okay," Adelita began.

Just then we were interrupted by a knock on the door. "That should be Señor Xiu," Adelita said. "I can explain everything upstairs. Tio Ignacio has some explaining to do for all of us."

"I should say so," I said as I went to the door. "Buenas tardes Hector," I said.

"Buenas tardes, Señora Canul," Señor Xiu said. "My son called me to come here. He said it was an emergency." Hector was obviously nervous. He had always been formal but calling me Señora Canul underlined his anxiety of showing up uninvited, especially after we had uninvited the Xiu's last time they came to our home.

We all turned to look at Adelita and Bembe.

"I think we need to go to the library," Adelita said. Adelita struggled to smile but couldn't get her mouth to change shape. She turned to climb the stairs. Bembe took the lead followed by Adelita.

We were almost to the library when we heard a loud pounding on the front door. Bembe and Adelita looked at each other. Adelita looked at me and shook her shoulders. I still had no idea what was going on. We turned to go back down the stairs.

I answered the door and K'abel Xiu pushed by me and shouted, "Hector, I know you are here. Your car is out front."

"I'm right here," Hector said. "I just got here. How did you know to come here? Did Bembe call you too?"

"Never mind how I knew," K'abel said. "You are here alone with this Canul woman. That is reason enough for me to be here."

"This Canul woman," I said, "just got here too, along with my mother. Your son is here, along with my daughter. We are trying to find out what is happening, just like you."

"Okay, now that everyone is here, let's go to the library and find out why," Adelita said.

Señor and Señora Xiu looked at each other, his raised eyebrows asking her, and she nodded yes. Everyone followed

Adelita and Bembe back to the library. Adelita said, "Okay Tio Ignacio, everyone is here but Papá. What do we do now?"

"Not everyone is here," Tio Ignacio said. "Where is your Abuela?"

"I am here Ignacio," Abuela said, out of breath from the climb up the stairs, being helped by Paco.

"Wait," Adelita said to her Abuela. "You can hear him? I thought only one person could hear him at a time." There was a pause and Adelita continued, "He says he usually only speaks to one person at a time, and on very rare occasions, he can speak to others."

K'abel and Hector had been quietly talking between themselves. They were talking in Yucatec Mayan. I only caught a word here and there. I smiled at the sound of it. Horado and I spoke Spanish to each other, but he didn't speak Mayan fluently. As I watched Adelita try to guide this conversation with Tio Ignacio and the Xiu family who knew nothing of the painting's abilities, my mind flashed to a conversation I had with Paco recently.

"I think I need to learn Mayan," Paco announced. "If I am going to be involved in the family business, and it is a Mayan business, then I should learn the language. All the shipping notes are in Mayan, plus the conversations Papá has with the shipper in Mexico is a mix of Spanish and Mayan."

"I hadn't thought of that," I admitted. "You are the first generation of our immediate family born and raised outside of Mexico. Our dialect of Mayan is not easy to learn, but if you work hard, you can learn it."

"Dialect?" Paco asked.

"There are eight Mayan languages, Paco," I explained. "They all originate from an original language of our ancestors. About six-million people speak a form of Mayan today. There were nearly two-hundred indigenous languages when the Spanish arrived in our lands. Many of these languages have disappeared.

There are about seventy languages still spoken in Mexico. You know, the funny thing is, almost all Mexicans can speak Spanish, but Spanish is not an official language recognized by the Mexican government. Just last year, the Mexican government officially adopted a dialect of the Aztec language, Nahuatl, as the country's official language because Spain refused to apologize on the 500th anniversary of the conquest of Mexico City. We are a people with long memories."

"And we have a rebellious streak in us that would make Crazy Horse proud," Paco said.

"Crazy Horse?" I asked. I had heard the name but didn't know much about this person.

"We studied him in school last year. He is a Native American, from here, not Mexico," Paco explained. "Ogallala Lakota tribe. He rebelled against the government back in the 1800's. He's famous for the Battle of the Little Big Horn. He would make any Toltec warrior proud. He was wise also. So much so he was feared by the government and was killed after surrendering."

"He sounds like a Benito Juárez," I suggested, and impressed with Paco's knowledge. "So tragic the history of countries."

"I'm guessing that is why what we do is so important," Paco said. "I'm new at this chocolate space stuff, but we can help avoid some of the tragedies, right? I was thinking the other day that we can tell stories of the decisions we helped improve, but that is what we can see. It's all the later decisions that are better by so many people who learned from that event that is the real power of what we do."

"We can't change the river flow with one decision, but we sure can over time," I said. "Even if we fail, and we do fail quite often, we have to trust in the simplicity of our mission. We can't make people change their minds and we don't get directly involved. I am still learning about trust after all these years of my involvement with the family business."

"Why don't people see what could be?" Paco asked.

"Hmm, maybe that is what we do, we create a space between stimulus and response, but we also improve eyesight," I said. "That reminds me of a story your Abuela told me when I was young. When the world was being formed, the first people were made of mud and God destroyed them because they had no brains, only heart. The second people were made of wood, but were found deficient because they had no emotions, only rationality, thus they could not praise God, nor be inspired."

"I have a few teachers that must have been made of wood," Paco said.

I ignored him and said, "The third people were made of corn. They could make the round trip between their heart and their head easily. God limited their vision so they couldn't see everything and had to depend on making that round trip for best decisions."

I don't remember what Paco said, if anything. I do remember his smile. He was really starting to understand not only how we do what we do, but why. Once again, I was humbled by the understanding of these people put in my care. Their title was "child," but they were showing themselves as leaders and wise doers.

Bringing myself back to the library and Adelita trying to find her way, with all of us in tow. I didn't know what was going on and why the entire Xiu family was again in my home, but Adelita was obviously in the driver's seat. I was uncomfortable with the situation, without Horado here. Adelita was trusting Tio Ignacio. I would trust him and Adelita. I smiled at my Mamá and she calmly nodded back. Maybe this was Tio Ignacio trying to get the Canul and the Xiu families back together, like my Mamá mentioned when we met Bembe.

Chapter Fourteen

"**W**HAT IS GOING ON?" LADY Xiu asked. "What Canul trickery is this? Bembe, what are you doing here?" K'abel was losing her composure. I was concerned she might actually hurt someone. Before I could say anything, Adelita held up her hand to quiet everyone. To my amazement, even K'abel stopped talking.

Adelita turned to K'abel and said, "Tio Ignacio has asked me to tell you to be patient and quiet for a change, like the time your Abuelo, asked you to not wake your mother. You wanted to open a birthday gift your mother had spent all night making. Just like the huipil, the shirt, your mother embroidered for you, you will get to unwrap this mystery too, if you are patient."

K'abel was so surprised she plopped down in my favorite chair without a word.

"I knew your grandfather," Abuela said. "I think I remember that blouse also. You have a good family, K'abel. Make them proud and be a good girl."

"Time is running out," Adelita announced. "There is a planned invasion of a corner of Belize from a group now assembling in Mexico. They want to start a new Mayan homeland in the area around the Milpas archeological site. Lady Xiu you know about this and who to call. You must tell those people that you demand to be present before they enter the Rio Bravo Conservation Area to claim their kingdom." Adelita was quiet and then continued. "You can promise to bring the rest of the Nobles to support their plan. They must not attack tonight. Tomorrow night is just as good, but you will bring greater support and a better chance of success."

K'abel Xiu was still speechless and didn't move from the chair.

"Mamá, Tio Ignacio says I must accompany Lady Xiu to Mexico," Adelita said. "The rebel Nobles are in a little town, not far from the Belize border, called Pioneros del Río Xnohá. We can drive there in a few hours from the Chetumal airport. We need be there tomorrow by midday, but we must leave now."

Still K'abel Xiu didn't say a word.

"I will have to go with you," I said. I had been willing to trust Tio Ignacio, but I wasn't prepared to send Adelita off to Mexico with K'abel. "Abuela," I asked my Mamá, "can you stay here to be with Paco?"

Adelita looked pale. I was just accepting this edict from Ignacio without question. I needed to understand what was really going on and why it had to be Adelita.

"Tio Ignacio says I have to go," Adelita said. "I'm the only person that will hear him in Mexico. He has to stay here, hanging on this wall. Abuela must accompany me. While in Mexico, Abuela, you will need to go to a Mayan artist and have your portrait painted. He says you will be needed here, for now, Mamá."

"I can hear you, Tio Ignacio," Abuela said. "I will take her. And, I know the artist you speak of," she added in a reverent tone.

"I will go," Lady Xiu said. "I find this entire plan ridiculous, but I do know who to call and I do think I can get them to wait for me to be there. For years they have been talking about this and I never thought they would actually do something. In the meantime, I can also contact the other Nobles. Not for support of the Milpas Plan, but to help stop it."

Faster than Paco disappears when it is time to wash the dishes, Adelita and her Abuela left for the airport and were on their way. I was nervous for Adelita and my Mamá, but I knew Mamá was wise, and she knew her way around Southern Mexico even better than the best tour guide. Lady Xiu was another matter.

I called Horado before we left for the airport. His phone went to voicemail. I was sure I couldn't trust K'abel Xiu. I wasn't sure I could trust Tio Ignacio. I knew I could trust my Mamá. I saw them off and tried to call Horado again. Voicemail.

"This is going to work out, Mamá," Paco said. Paco had been mostly quiet during all of this, and I had almost forgotten he was sitting by me in the car as my mind raced from Adelita to my Mamá and then to an invasion. I had just sent the two ladies in my life into that crazy environment. "There was a reason you were not supposed to travel with Adelita and Abuela, but that doesn't mean we should just sit around here. Papá is already in Mexico. I think we should go visit him."

We were still on Century Boulevard, just leaving the airport. I pulled into the McDonalds parking lot instead of getting on the 405 Freeway. I turned and looked at Paco. "Why do you think we should go to Mexico?" I asked. "Maybe there is something we can do from here that we can't do from there."

"Mamá, it's a blessing to have Tio Ignacio in our family business," Paco said. "I don't know how all that works, but he helps us a lot. Could we do it without him? Sure. Maybe not as well, but we could still make and deliver chocolates. No offense to him, but we are a family first, chocolate space makers second. When family intersects with our job, we both know which takes priority."

"You are right Paco," I said, somewhat stunned. "Which one of us is the parent?"

"You are the parent, Mamá," Paco said with a smile. "Whatever you decide I will follow. "I'm just a know-it-all teenager offering my advice, no rhymes, but I hope with reason."

"Your advice is Mexico?" I asked, trying to settle it in my own head.

"I have been preparing for something," Paco said. "I haven't known what and maybe this isn't it, but I am ready, as best a person my age and capabilities can be anyway."

"It isn't like you might think," I said. "This isn't going to be a school ground fútbol game or even a close contact basketball game. I am afraid. Afraid for you, for Adelita, Abuela, and what we might get into that we can't get out of." I admitted.

"Mamá, a few weeks ago I nearly got in a fight at school" Paco said.

"Is that what happened?" I asked. "I remember you saying something, but it felt like the conversation was closed before it started, so I didn't push it. Maybe I should have."

"Xavier, a boy I've known since first grade picked a fight with me. I think it was part of a gang initiation. Xavier had to show his allegiance to his new friends by fighting someone. Either he or the gang picked me because I had shunned the gang. It didn't seem like that big of a deal at the time, because I still felt something bigger was going to happen. I have been preparing for a long time."

"Preparing?" I asked.

"I don't play much basketball anymore" Paco said with a quiet smile. "I have been working out, reading, praying, thinking. I am not a martial arts expert, but I have been working on personal defense too."

"So, what happened?" I asked as I realized again how much I didn't know about Paco and the burdens he has been carrying.

"I don't mind getting roughed up, but I didn't want to worry you, Mamá," Paco said as his dark brown eyes watched me for a sign whether he would decide to continue. I smiled at him, and he smiled back.

"I tried to avoid Xavier after school, but I walked right into an ambush. So much for trying to be observant and avoiding danger. Anyway, four boys older than me that I didn't know surrounded me and then pushed Xavier into the circle. I noticed two other boys watching for police or school officials since we were by the west side outdoor basketball courts. I realized this was going to get serious and I was in real trouble. More trouble than maybe a black eye."

I kept quiet as Paco talked but I wanted to scream or take my little boy in my arms or find those boys and beat them up myself. I just stared at Paco, urging him to continue.

"Everyone was taunting Xavier. I knew I was just the punching bag. I was going to let Xavier beat me up and get this over with. I knew I could probably fight and win, but that would just cause more problems. The gang would then attack me, and I could get really hurt. I wasn't sure what to do until Xavier attacked."

"It was crazy, but somehow, I caught Xavier's fist with my left hand, sort of like catching his fist like a baseball. That surprised me more than it did Xavier. I held Xavier's right fist and pivoted away from a wide left swing by Xavier's left fist. It was like everything was in slow motion. I felt stronger and stronger as I kept trying to avoid the punches. I wasn't running away, but I wasn't attacking either. There were times when I had opportunities to hit back but never took them. I knew I was lucky, or maybe protected, but not a single hard punch hit me. The other boys became more and more quiet. I didn't know if that was good or bad. Soon they stopped taunting and just watched. Xavier was at first embarrassed and then mad, and finally, quiet himself."

"I looked at Xavier, trying to call a truce with my eyes and his stare went from enemy to some sort of unspoken respect. It was now or never for me to get out of that place, so I stooped down to pick up my books, thinking that would be the moment I would get kicked or jumped on. Nothing happened. I nodded my head at Xavier and walked away. I didn't start running until I turned the corner, out of sight of the gang. I wasn't afraid of those boys. I didn't run to get away, okay I probably was," Paco said with another more open smile, "but I was also running to something. I wasn't sure what until today. I had been prepared but I also knew I had been super lucky. That crazy display wouldn't happen a second time. I had to think of other ways to avoid the gangs and their dumb fights. But I am running to this fight Mamá. I know I am still a dumb little kid in some ways and there are a lot of things I don't understand. But I am not unprepared."

I was in awe mostly at his humility. I wasn't sure what to say. I wanted to change his school, hire a bodyguard, but all I said was, "So you are alright?"

"I'm fine Mamá," Paco answered.

"So, Mexico?" I asked again.

"Papá is already there. I don't know what we can do, but it will be a lot clearer there, than here. The house is locked up. You know where Papá is. Let's go to him. He will know where Adelita and Abuela are heading."

"Pioneros del Río Xnohá," I repeated. "Let's do this. We will have to go home. We need our passports. I will get those. You grab different shoes and a long-sleeve shirt. Those flip flops and T-shirt aren't proper jungle attire"

We were home and back on the road to the airport in record time. I was grateful once again for where we lived. By the time we parked and went to the ticket counter, the flight my Mamá and Adelita were on was already gone. Too late for us. Just as well. As we were trying to decide which flight to take, Horado called back.

"Sorry Querida," Horado began. "I forgot to bring a cell phone charger. I just barely bought one. I didn't know you had called. Is something going on? I will be back tomorrow."

I explained what had happened and where Adelita and Mamá were heading. "What should we do? We want to travel right now to join up with you." I held my breath waiting for his reply.

Without a single commentary on the craziness of all this he simply said, "Take the flight to Campeche. That will shave a couple hours off going to Merida. I will start driving now and meet you and Paco in Xpujil. Let's meet at the base de taxis. There is only one in town, and everyone knows where it is if you have to ask directions. You will find the town on the map, along the Villahermosa-Chetumal highway. I think it is the México 186. It has tolls, so get some pesos at the airport."

I wanted to tell Horado about Paco's wisdom, but it could wait. We had a flight to catch. We landed in Campeche eight and a half hours later, because we had to switch aircraft in Mexico City. I was exhausted. Paco was able to sleep during both flights. It didn't appear that any of this was troubling him very much. *Tal palo, tal estilo.* Like father, like son.

We rented a car and were on our way. I missed a turn in Escárcega, but we made good time and I found the taxi stand in Xpujil at 6:30 in the morning. I parked across the street at the Abarrotes, the little grocery store for this sleepy town. The smell of the freshly made tortillas from the shop was intoxicating. I bought some still hot corn tortillas and Paco and I enjoyed them for breakfast. I leaned my seat back and closed my eyes. I asked Paco to keep an eye out for his Papá. I was awoken a few minutes later by a tap on the car window. I opened my eyes to see Horado smiling at me. Paco was sawing logs. I looked at my watch. 8:47. I had been asleep for two hours.

"Querida, bienvenido a México," Horado said with enthusiasm. "Have you been waiting long?"

"Not long enough," I said. "It feels like I just closed my eyes. I got out of the car and shut the door quietly so I wouldn't wake up Paco. I told Horado about Paco's counsel and support. "He is definitely the best of both of us, Horado. He could be treating this as just an adventure, but he has a caution about him that goes beyond my anxieties and your jump then grow wings attitude."

"Paco is a good boy. He takes after his Mamá more than me. Speaking of wings," Horado said, "I rented this van knowing where we were headed, there would be no place to sleep. I don't want to bring any attention to ourselves by asking around for a place to eat and sleep. Let's find a safe place to park your car."

"No need to," I said. "We rented from Explora specifically because I can turn it in here in case we needed to. They open at nine, about now. It costs an additional day of rent to turn it in here, but its only 126 pesos a day plus gas."

"Excellente," Horado said. "You are too hard on yourself. Paco gets his wisdom from you. I never would have thought of that. Let's get the car turned in and get on the road. We can talk after that."

As it turned out, the rental agency was just down the road. We were heading for Pioneros del Río Xnohá by 9:30. "It's a two-hour drive to Pioneros," Horado said. "We can eat an early lunch after we get there. The food is in the ice chest."

"What is all this other stuff?" Paco asked from the back seat.

"Things we might need," Horado said. "I quietly asked around about what is going on down here. There are between fifty and one-hundred men gathered in Pioneros. They are armed and looking for a fight. It's more than talk. They really plan to march into Belize and claim a large area, about 100 square miles, for a new Mayan kingdom. They expect support by the locals who feel forgotten by the Belize government. La Milpa, the archeological site there, will be their capital. They have prepared a marketing campaign to launch tomorrow that will garner, they hope, international support from other indigenous rights groups. Far from actually fighting for rights, they are setting up a feudal kingdom with an aristocracy, a small merchant middle class and mostly agricultural workers whose life probably won't change much, at least not for the better."

"Have they considered what the British did the last time they were attacked in a remote corner of the world, by a group that figured they would just let it happen?" I asked.

"The Malvinas War?" Paco asked.

Horado and I were surprised by his insight. "That's right, I said. Don't' tell me you learned that in school last year too."

"No, I learned it this year," Paco said. "YouTube videos. Easy guess. The British don't go around attacking remote places these days."

Horado smiled at Paco. I think they did a virtual high five with their eyes. Horado continued, "Belize got its independence from Great Britain in 1981 or 1982. The same time as the Falklands Malvinas War. The British still maintain troops in the country to protect against invasions from Guatemala. I expect a tiny invasion force from Mexico would be considered the same."

"The Malvinas War only lasted two months and that was against the country of Argentina, as you know" Horado added. "I doubt it would take two weeks to wipe out this invasion plan."

"So, Adelita and my Mamá are walking into a group of crazy people who really aren't thinking this through," I said, feeling my anxiety grow.

"Not to mention K'abel Xiu," Horado said. "From what I gathered, K'abel's younger sister is one of the rebel leaders. Family feuds can be the worst."

"So, what can we do?" I asked. "Can we find Adelita and Mamá and rescue them?"

"Let's get to Pioneros del Río Xnohá and see what's going on," Horado said. "We will know better what we can do when we have better information."

We drove in silence for about an hour more. The deep jungle had almost no human footprint that I could see. A fire, or the smoke from a fire is all I saw that suggested there was anything other than primeval jungle engulfing us. We drove on. According to the map Horado had, this is where the proverbial road ended. I didn't like the feeling nor the connotation of the end of the road.

Horado pulled off the road by a small river just short of the town. He said, "I will go scout out the village and who is here. I will be back in half an hour. If I don't return, stay hidden for an hour more and then head back the way you came. If there is a problem, let's meet in Campeche."

"Should I go with you?" Paco asked.

"I would feel better if you watched over your Mamá," Horado answered. "I won't do anything foolish, don't you either."

Horado got out of the van and walked down a path leading to the village. He disappeared in the undergrowth in less than a minute. "Could I finish up the tortillas? Paco asked. "I'm hungry."

I handed him the tortillas I had in the front seat after offering them to Horado. I wondered how he could eat. My stomach was tied up in knots tighter than the weave of a Jippi Jappa basket. I half expected rebels to surround the van. Nothing happened. Horado was back in less than half an hour.

"Lots going on and nothing at all," Horado said getting back into the van. "There are eighty to a hundred men gathered on the other side of town. They have ATVs, handheld weapons, and supplies, but they don't look like an invasion force. They are camped in a small, sloped field, kind of like an outdoor amphitheater. They have a makeshift stage area at the bottom of the field. Great undergrowth cover on all sides. Maybe they have plans to be resupplied after a few days. No sign of your Mamá, Adelita, or K'abel Xiu. There are plenty of strangers in town. I didn't stick out."

"What's our next step?" I asked.

"It's nearly eleven," Horado said looking at his watch. "Past lunchtime at home. I think we should eat."

"Eat?" I asked incredulously. "Adelita is out in this jungle. Those men have guns and evil on their minds. And you want to eat?"

"Nothing is going to happen in the next hour, probably nothing until tonight," Horado said.

His patience with my impatience made me madder.

"I want us to set up where the main group is located. There are several stands of trees and brush where we can be close but go completely undetected. This might be the last time we get a chance to eat until tomorrow."

Horado was right, but I changed the subject. "Was there any place that the three of them could be staying in the village?"

"I didn't see a single possibility," Horado said. "I didn't want to ask too many questions. I asked if they had seen three female outsiders. I told them I was looking for my wife. The locals are keeping their distance from the rebels. I am sure the people I spoke with considered me one of the rebels, so they may have not answered my questions with all the information they might have. I suppose there could be a small home that K'abel could have set up for them to stay."

"I say we eat and stake out a place where we can see what's going on," Paco said. "I'm tired of wondering and waiting."

"We will be doing a lot more waiting I am afraid," Horado said. "At least we will be where we will know what's going on. If they are here, or if they arrive sometime today, we will be in a better place to know."

"And then what?" I asked. "How are we going to keep them safe from this little army?"

"I came prepared," Horado said. "Those boxes that you asked about earlier Paco, let's go through them while we eat."

"Okay fine, let's eat," I said. "I want to get going too."

Horado opened up an ice chest. I was expecting sandwiches. We ate chips, guacamole, and a fruit gazpacho made up of cucumbers. jicama. mango. watermelon. papaya. and pineapple, topped with Tajin chili powder. Not exactly a solid meal, but with the heat, humidity, and no air conditioning, it was great. I hoped we would be able to eat again before tomorrow. Then again, the longer I went without finding Adelita and Mamá, the less hungry I felt.

While we ate, Horado opened the other boxes in the back of the van. "I picked up some black long-sleeved shirts for both of you. That will protect you from insects and help keep us hidden if it comes to that. Even in the daylight, we will be part of the shadows. Put some dirt on your face too. You don't need to cover your faces but removing the shininess from oils on your faces will help. Enough of our defense. Let's talk offense."

"I don't want to cause any problems we can't get out of," I said. "Let's protect Adelita and Mamá."

"And Lady Xiu," Paco added.

"And Lady Xiu," I said. "I just don't want to fix all the issues. We aren't here to stop an invasion."

"Your daughter is here for that, as I understand it from your explanation," Horado said. "I agree, we aren't here looking for a fight. I brought some things that will be helpful, depending on what happens. Don't worry, there is nothing deadly."

"Don't get me wrong, Horado," I amended. "I will do whatever it takes to keep our ladies safe. I just can't believe I let this happen in the first place. I mean, I just let my daughter and not so young Mamá head to the jungle to interrupt an invasion. I worry every morning letting her walk to school on her own."

"She's got me to watch over her, to school and now here," Paco said. "What do you have for us, Papá?"

"These," Horado said. He pulled out some long metal tubes and started putting them together.

"Blow guns?" I asked.

"Yep," Horado said. "And darts with a mild tranquilizer. They should put a man to sleep for a few hours." He completed putting the first one together. It was about four feet long, had a mouthpiece at one end, and he connected ten darts on holders around the gun.

"Be careful to not touch the tips of the darts when you load them," Horado said, handing it to Paco. "This isn't like the blowgun I've let you play around with at home." He put another one together and set it aside.

"I don't get a gun?" I asked, knowing I wouldn't. I hated the things, and he knew it. Horado was a champion blowgun hunter. I have put up with them our entire married life, but I wanted no part of them.

"I brought these for you," he said, handing me what looked like a pistol. "It's a pulse taser. It's good up to fifteen feet. It will demobilize a person for about 30 seconds. It's so you can protect us from anyone trying to locate us. Paco and I will be focused on those who might be a threat to Adelita."

I held the taser and shot it in a direction away from Horado and Paco. It made a little pop but nothing loud or identifiable.

"I also brought these. They are Wi-Fi speakers and we each have a mic wirelessly connected to each one. We will set the speakers in locations away from us but will be able to talk like we have a megaphone. This is just in case we need to communicate to the rebels."

We loaded everything up in some camo backpacks and left the van. I added to my worries that someone would find it and either take it or disable it and we would be stranded here.

We were just out of site of the van and Horado turned to us. "From here on out, let's keep talk to emergencies. I don't want to call any attention to ourselves. I walked into town before. Now I want to avoid it and set ourselves up where the invasion group is located. If Adelita shows up, that is where she will go, or where Tio Ignacio will direct her."

The campsite where about sixty men were sitting around came into view a few minutes later. This really was a small village. It was two in the afternoon. It was hot, humid, and the bugs were terrible. I was glad I had on a long sleeve shirt, but I was extra hot because of it. We settled into some undergrowth and Horado pulled out a mosquito netting for me.

"Get a little rest," Horado whispered. "It looks like the group is pretty confident about their safety. There are no perimeter guards or patrols that I can see, but you never know. I am going to place the speakers before it gets dark." Turning to Paco he said, "Paco, stay alert and watch for any movement or changes to let me know about when I get back."

In seconds he was gone, disappearing into the jungle. Horado was concerned for Adelita and my Mamá, but I could tell he was also enjoying this. I was simultaneously grateful Horado was in his element and upset because the rest of all I loved in this world was here too.

"Mamá," I heard Paco say in my ear. I opened my eyes, and it was dark out. I could barely make out his face next to me. He didn't say anymore, just pointed to the large campfire in the opening. There were more people, maybe eighty all standing or sitting around, obviously waiting for something or someone. I couldn't see Horado. I wanted to ask where he was, but decided if Paco wasn't concerned, I wouldn't be either.

I noticed a few rebels at the back of the group. They were walking the perimeter of the open area. They were as startled as I was when someone by the campfire called everyone to attention. No one stood up at attention, or put their hands to their sides, but they all turned to look. I recognized the speaker as the sister of K'abel Xiu. I couldn't remember her name, but she was as striking as her sister, in beauty and command.

"Army of the Kingdom of La Milpa," K'abel's sister said in a loud voice. "The time has come. Early tomorrow morning, before the sun comes up, we will be on the trail to our destiny. At one time in our history, Calakmul went to war against Tikal. Today we have the blood of both great kingdoms running in our blood. Tomorrow night, La Milpa will be ours. All of Mayan descent will be welcome in the First Kingdom since the Spanish overthrew Nojpeten, capital of the Itzas Mayans. That was in 1697. You will be able to tell your grandchildren that you were the first generation since then to claim your legacy."

I couldn't believe my ears. These people were living in a fantasy world. The idea of a gathering place for the Maya sounded exciting but giving up our ancestral homes to take one by force was not the way. I turned to look for Horado again, to see his reaction to this speech. I couldn't see him, but I saw movement near another trail coming from the west. My heart stopped. It was Adelita, alone. Before I could move toward her, she was spotted by that soldier that kept an eye on the perimeter of the encampment.

She was grabbed from behind and yanked off her feet. "Who are you and who are you whispering to?" the soldier asked. "Do you have a radio? Who were you talking to?"

He didn't wait for an answer. He pulled Adelita out into the encampment and directly to K'abel's sister. The speech-making stopped and so did my breathing. I looked around and this time I saw Horado motioning to me to stay down. He was watching what was going on but did not appear terrified. I wanted to slug him in the arm. Our little girl had been captured by these lunatics.

"What is a little girl doing in the jungle?" K'abel's sister asked the man who had grabbed her. I was wondering where my Mamá was, and K'abel.

"She was whispering to someone, but I couldn't find anyone. No radio or other communications device, no identification. Just this backpack and the only thing in it is chocolate. Maybe she is crazy," the guard reported.

K'abel's sister asked Adelita something in a Mayan dialect she didn't understand.

"I speak English and Spanish," Adelita said with very little fear in her voice. I was astounded. I had enough fear for the both of us.

"Who are you and what are you doing here?" K'abel's sister asked again in Spanish.

"I am Adelita Canul," Adelita said. "I came here with my Abuela and Lady K'abel Xiu to talk with you."

K'abel's sister recognized Lady Xiu's name. "Where are they at? Is that who you were talking to when you got caught?"

"They are asleep in Xkan," Adelita said. "We got in late, and we were going to walk here in the morning. I walked through the jungle by myself to talk to you."

"Why are you here now, in the middle of the night? K'abel's sister asked.

Adelita took a breath and said, "My Tio Ignacio woke me up. He told me to walk here."

"And where is your Tio?" K'abel's sister asked, losing patience.

"He is in Los Angeles, California. Well, actually, I think he is buried here in Mexico."

I thought of Mamá and K'abel. They were going to wake up in a few hours and find Adelita gone. Surely, they wouldn't have planned to send her out alone. I had no idea how we were going to rescue Adelita, but I was grateful we were here. And then I looked at Adelita. A little girl, in a foreign land with very dangerous people.

"There is a place," Mamá told me when I was young, "called Xibalba which I think in English you would say "place of fright." It's entrance, the stories say, is in a cave in what is now Belize. This place is ruled by powerful kings known as the Lords of Xibalba. It was a terrible place."

I looked at Adelita, surrounded by these people, lusting for power and violence. This was certainly a place of fright. Yet, Adelita did not appear to be afraid. Far from that, in fact. She stood like a warrior among warriors, without fear and without shame. I would not have been surprised had she sprouted wings and began to fly.

Then I remembered more of the story Mamá had shared with me. "The hero twins, Hunahpu and Xbalanque overcame the Lords of Xibalba," Mamá explained. "They did so with their complementary forces. They represented sky and earth, day and night. Some say they were male and female."

I knew there was more to the story, but all I could think of was Adelita standing in the midst of these Lords of Xibalba, and Paco by my side, confident and ready to protect his sister.

Chapter Fifteen

"**T**HIS IS NOT A GAME, Señorita Canul," K'abel's sister said. "Tell me the truth, now, or I will lock you up and throw away the key."

"I have told you the complete truth," Adelita said. "I would not have walked through the jungle in the middle of the night, in a place I have never been, into the hands of mean people, for a game or a joke. You are in big trouble, and you don't know it. That is why I am here."

"We are in big trouble?" K'abel's sister asked with a laugh. "You are the one in trouble, very big trouble. I hope you haven't made any plans for your Quinceanera."

"I am twelve," Adelita said. "I've got time. But you don't. I have no idea what your plans are, except that you plan to build a little kingdom in a corner of Belize, but I know Lady Xiu will come looking for me. You need to wait until then."

"Lock her up!" K'abel's sister said. "I think you are right Pablo; she is nuts."

"I am not nuts," Adelita yelled, "but you are if you go into Belize. There is an Army training exercise, that includes British soldiers, going on by the Milpa Archaeological site. Many of you will be killed."

"Get her out of my site," K'abel's sister said. "She is making stuff up just to create doubts. I am sure my sister put her up to it. She never had a stomach for the real destiny of the Nobles. Get some rest. We move out at dawn."

"But what if she or your sister are telling the truth?" the man who caught Adelita asked.

"We are not far, maybe twenty miles from the Maya Biosphere Reserve in Guatemala," K'abel's sister said. She turned to Adelita and said, "If you are a Canul, your distant cousins lived there, but past Guatemalan government plans moved them out, forcibly. This and other reasons are why we will establish a Mayan kingdom in our homelands. If we have to do this by force, so be it. Take her away. Now."

"Come on Akna, you know as well as I do," a voice behind the crowd of men and women interjected, "that you are only interested in yourself and want to place yourself at the top of the social and economic pyramid, amidst our ancestors' pyramids."

I turned to see who was speaking. K'abel Xiu entered from the same trail that Adelita had come from. She walked into the light of the campfire. She looked commanding and in charge, rather than her demeaning and aloof self. She stared down everyone who was looking at her with her laser eyes. It took her younger sister, the person who had been questioning Adelita, a minute to compose herself.

"So, I was right, this was K'abel's sister," I said out loud. I put my hand over my mouth, for fear I spoke too loud. Fortunately, I had been drowned out by K'abel's command.

"Adelita, come here, now," K'abel ordered like she was in trouble. I was about to stand up and run to my daughter, but Paco put his hand on my arm.

"Akna, and all the rest of you so called Nobles, what are you doing?" K'abel continued. "Do you think this is the year 1500 and you are going to try to kick the Spanish out of your territory? You are all going to end up in jail, if you're not killed."

"We don't need your lecture K'abel," Akna said. "You said you would be able to add to our army if we waited a day. We waited. Where are your soldiers?"

"I spoke with every other Noble, K'abel said. "They want no part in this."

Paco nudged me again. I had thought he was keeping me from standing up, but he was signaling to me that Horado and he were about to go on the offensive. While everyone was focused on the family feud between K'abel and Akna, including me, Horado had started shooting darts. Already several of the soldiers at the back of the crowd were falling or sitting down and then crumbling to the ground.

K'abel Xiu kept talking. Everyone kept looking at her. Paco lifted his blow gun and sent a dart to the man closest to us. The dart hit its intended target, but the soldier swatted at it like a mosquito had bit him. A second dart hit him, this time in the neck. He sat down and then he laid down like he was going to sleep. He was out. As the man near him turned to see what the movement was, Paco hit him with a dart. K'abel's voice again caught my attention.

"If you must," K'abel continued, "send out a small group of your best soldiers. Have them report back to you what is going on in your targeted corner of Belize. Your lives are worth the wait, no?"

The number of soldiers and leaders listening continued to shrink. Paco and Horado were picking them off one-by-one. Finally, someone noticed. "Akna, something is happening right here," a soldier yelled. Pedro Esquivel was standing right by me and now he is sleeping. So are others." Everyone turned to look around.

"Someone has poisoned us," another soldier yelled.

Akna and K'abel were both surprised. I could tell this hadn't been part of K'abel Xiu's plan. I thought she might have found Horado, and she was a diversionary tactic with her speech. Now I could tell she was scared. She grabbed her sister and tried to run. They didn't get very far. Akna tripped and fell to the ground. I looked at Paco and he pumped his arm and smiled.

"That is far enough," Horado's voice called in Spanish from the jungle. "Don't run, you'll miss all the fun," Paco then said in English. This was the first time in this crazy night that Adelita looked surprised. I saw two soldiers who tried to get away and they only made it three steps before they fell to the ground.

"Everyone put your weapons by the campfire, then step back and sit down," I called out, surprised I could sound so confident. I saw Adelita mouth, "Mamá?' A soldier tossed his rifle by the fire and turned to back away. He fell to the ground. "I said all your weapons. That soldier has a knife and a pistol hidden under his shirt. If you want the same thing to happen to you, do as he did." I had no idea if that soldier really did have other weapons, but I was trying to put fear in everyone. This really was becoming a place of fright, but not an evil fright. My heroic twins, even though they were born years apart, were overcoming the evil of this place.

By now every soldier was scared and leaving all their weapons by the fire. Two more fell trying to leave during the commotion. One had tried to leave near where I was hidden. I tased him and he fell with a yell. That added to the fear. I could tell that K'abel was now petrified. She finally got her courage back and yelled into the jungle, "Show yourselves. We mean you no harm."

"You meant to say, "you have no means to do us any harm,"" Horado called back. "Young lady, yes you Adelita Canul, get your bag of chocolates."

Adelita ran to the soldier that had taken it from her. He bent down and handed it to Adelita quickly wanting no part of this. She brought it closer to the campfire. "I have it," Adelita called back, holding it up.

"Give a piece to everyone who has made the wise choice to cooperate," Horado said. Adelita started to hand out the chocolate. I wondered how Horado knew her bag had chocolate in it. Then I remember Paco filling her backpack with chocolate before she left. I was in shock mode at the time, barely able to breath, let alone think of this future scenario. "Take a minute and eat the chocolate you have been given," Paco called out and continued. "As you chew it, think of your ancestors, think of your families now. Consider that this is the last meal you will ever eat in this life." Horado and Paco were quiet and all I could hear were people chewing. Some had their eyes closed. Some were sobbing. Some were smiling.

"You were saying, Lady Xiu?" Horado asked as everyone, including her, finished their chocolate.

"I was saying you should show yourself," K'abel said, her voice shaking.

"In due time," Horado said. "What were you saying before that? It sounded very wise."

"I was saying that this plan to create a kingdom in the jungle of Belize was foolish. The Nobles want no part of this. Actually, this small group is alone in the entire world. No one wants to be a part of this, except perhaps the well trained and armed soldiers on the other side of the border who are ready and willing to protect their country."

I watched the words and the chocolate be absorbed by the soldiers who only minutes ago were ready to attack another country. They were thoughtful, even peaceful. Many hung their heads down, others just sat down. It wasn't pricks of darts that were subduing them, but their own better decisions.

"It's time to go home," Horado said. "It's time to create your Mayan homeland in your own homes. Teach your children their heritage. Treat them to Mayan chocolate and your wise presence, instead of your lack of being with them because you were killed or are in jail. It's time to go home."

A soldier got up and at first was afraid to take a step. "Go home," Paco commanded in Spanish. The soldier took one step, then a second one and soon got in a car with six others who crammed in, and they drove away. Others followed. Soon there were only about ten or twelve soldiers standing around. They looked lost, or unsure what to do. Adelita gave them the last of her chocolate. They thanked her and one called out, "We are from Belize. We were recruited to help guide this army to their goal, the Milpa Archaeological site. What should we do?"

"Go home," Horado said again. "In small groups you will be safe. If you meet up with soldiers, you will not appear as a threat. Offer them your chocolate and you will make a friend instead of an enemy. This is your final invitation. Go home or meet the same fate as your fellow soldiers."

They all left and only Adelita and K'abel Xiu were standing by the fire. It was silent. Neither of them were sure what to do. They looked at each other, then K'abel looked down at her sister, crumpled on the ground. K'abel started crying. Adelita went over to her, opened her arms, and she fell into them.

"You smell really good," I heard Adelita say to K'abel. That's my daughter, I thought. She just faced down an invasion army and she says whatever comes to her mind.

"A woman of culture does not attend a failed invasion without her favorite perfume," K'abel said trying to sound lighthearted. She was shaking now.

"Everything will be alright," I heard myself saying. "They will all wake up in about four hours with crazy strong headaches, but that will pass quickly. We will keep an eye out for them until they wake up. We don't want jaguar or army ants to come and drag them away. They should be fine as long as the fire keeps going."

"Can you show yourself now?" K'abel asked. The jungle was completely silent. Horado had obviously decided not to show ourselves. I was pretty certain Adelita recognized our voices, but K'abel had not. I think Horado felt it better to leave it like that.

I watched Adelita and K'abel sit by the fire for a few minutes and K'abel gathered her whits and finally she said, "Let's get back to that shack your Abuela calls a hotel before she wakes up. I didn't leave her a note. Did you?"

"No, I had to leave too quickly," Adelita explained. "I think the invaders were getting ready to leave and I guess I was needed to stall them. How did you know to come here?"

"I woke up," K'abel said as she walked down the path, not more than ten feet from where I was hidden. She suddenly turned back to Adelita and added, "Actually a voice woke me up and it told me to follow you. I thought, Adelita is asleep in the other room. The voice said, go outside and see, so I did. I saw you get some things out of the car and leave. I thought I was out of my mind to follow you, but I was worried about you. I wanted to stop you and tell you to go back to the hotel, but instead, for some crazy reason, I did what the voice said, and I followed you. You were very brave to tell them what you did. I couldn't let you stand up to them alone. I didn't have a plan though. Was whoever else was there, part of your plan?"

My heart was overflowing with gratefulness for K'abel and what I guessed was Tio Ignacio. Again, I had the impulse to stand up and run to Adelita. Paco placed his hand on my arm again. I looked at him this time and he put his finger to his lips.

Adelita said, "I was just following what Tio Ignacio told me to do. I was scared, but I didn't think they were going to hurt me. I never saw who those voices were or how they got here. Maybe Tio Ignacio has his own army," Adelita added.

I was touched by Adelita's presence of mind. She should be in shock, but she was following Horado's lead without even seemingly thinking about it.

"Whoever it was, saved the day," K'abel said, starting to walk down the trail again, and putting her arm around Adelita.

"They sure did, but you were the hero too," Adelita added. "You stood up to the leader who I guess is your sister?"

"My baby sister," K'abel said. "If you think I'm hard to get along with, you ought to share a bedroom with her. She is a good person, except for invading countries here and there," she added now sounding more lighthearted.

I don't know what else they said as they walked down that trail. Horado put some more large logs on the fire. He and Paco pulled the sleeping men closer to the fire and stacked their weapons. All three of us collected every dart we could find. We left the camp about thirty minutes after Adelita and K'abel and walked back to our rented van in silence.

Once we were in the van, I asked, "Do we go find Adelita now?"

"They have other plans," Horado said. "Remember, your Mamá was to travel to Telchaquillo to meet with the man that is to paint her picture. That is about seven hours from here. They have another long day ahead of themselves. For whatever reason, we were not invited to that event. I assume Adelita will get a tour our ancestral lands. If not, we will come back as a family."

"Maybe with the Xiu family too," Paco said.

"How do you know where Mamá is to go for her portrait?" I asked.

"It's something Tio Ignacio let slip some years ago," Horado said, shrugging his shoulders. "He mentioned something about when he sat for his portrait."

I dropped the subject because I didn't want to talk about the implications for my Mamá's future. I was also frustrated anew that I seem to always be left out of family insights. Why did Tio Ignacio share that with Horado and not me? I know it's not about me, so now I feel extra frustrated. Not for the first time I was in that twilight zone of gratefulness and hurt, bright future and feeling left out. I focused on the positive side of my world.

We drove straight to Cancun. It was a six-hour drive, but we were able to catch a nonstop flight into LAX. I have no idea how Horado stayed awake through the whole drive. I slept on the drive but couldn't get to sleep on the plane. Horado was asleep before we taxied out of parking. We were at home by mid-afternoon.

It was great to be home, but the house felt empty without Adelita. Horado and Paco went to bed early, but I still couldn't sleep, so I went up to the library to read. I stared at Tio Ignacio's painting. "I suppose you are a Mayan mask," I told him. "You are painted to catch the eye and hide what is beneath, no?"

Like most masks, it didn't answer. The person, the whatever that was beneath the mask chose not to answer. That reminded me of *Rabinal Achí*. It is an ancient Mayan play that has been performed every year in Rabinal, Guatemala. I attended one time, in January, when I was at the university. Its original name was Xajoj Tun, meaning "Dance of the Trumpet." The play centers around a historical feud between Rabinal and K'iche', two neighboring cities. While the cast includes the entire village, only five of these characters speak. Because of the masks, all the speaking parts could be done by two people.

Two princes confront each other while dancers move in a circle. The dialogue also goes in a circle. The speaking characters repeat part of the speech of the person who just spoke. Phrases such as, "Is this not what you have just said?" try to confirm or establish a compromise. The other person will then speak and usually ratify the other person's point with words like, "Thus you spoke." In a way, the play is very slow, and it appears there is not a lot of action or progress toward a conclusion. It certainly doesn't follow the template of a Hollywood blockbuster.

The play is amazing though. The hundreds of masks of all the performers are ancient and are great works of art. New masks are made by artisans who do their work in secret. No one knows who they are. The circles, both danced and spoken, are reminiscent of Ajmac, from the Mayan calendar and our family symbol. The swirl that helps people try to prevent mistakes. The center point of the swirl, the waring princes of the Xajoj Tun, represents the mind in contemplation, thinking. The outer swirl, the masked dancers of the Xajoj Tun, dressed as animals, spirits, people, or elements of the natural world, represent all the possible outcomes. The three lines going in different directions represent wise decisions. It also means wisdom, sincere study, humility, so a person can learn something new. It is interesting that the play is performed every year. I suppose that is to keep its words and choreography fresh in the minds of each generation, but maybe also to remind everyone of its lessons. We all need repetition and practice to help us on our journey.

It is the masks that hold the mystery. They are the veil between the world as we see it and the world beyond. Without the masks, we would recognize the face of the dancers or the waring princes as our next-door neighbor, the man who works at the tortilla factory, or the woman who sells flowers on the street corner. With the masks, things can be said, messages received, and meaning made, that otherwise would be difficult if not impossible.

They represent more than the story's characters. The masks are considered sacred, as the dancers connect with the *rajawales* (energies of the dead characters the actors and dancers represent) through them. Mamá told me that her Mamá told her that a special ritual is practiced with the masks, called "The Vigil of the Masks". During the ritual the participants offer *pom* (incense), they pray, light candles, and abstain from certain actions and foods to invoke the energy of the dancers who have passed. We practice respect for Tio Ignacio. Good heavens, on his word I sent my 12-year-old daughter with her Abuela to quell an invasion in another country.

The artisans who paint the masks, or the portraits of Tio Ignacio, my Mamá, and others, are the real bridges, the prophets between what could or will be, and our realities. I took in a quick breath as a sudden thought surfaced. Horado wanted to paint my Mamá and now she is being painted by some mystery artist. Is there a connection? Will Horado's future swirls of his paint brushes create a painting that can not only communicate, but know things that are unknowable? Is Horado a future prophet artisan?

A prophet needs a source, or they are just a charlatan. What is the source of Tio Ignacio? Is it God? Is it an angel of God? Is it the light, the word, the truth that God has declared? Is it our ancestors? Is it someone alive today using this medium to communicate while maintaining a shroud of anonymity? If I didn't believe in God, would I say, there is just a person behind the mask. There is just a person behind the painting, and its ability to communicate can be explained by science. Thus, the prophet, if you want to call a person by that title, is the person who hears the message of the mask, or the painting, not the creator of the veil.

'Today, Adelita is our prophetess,' I thought to myself. Not long ago it was Horado, and before him, me. And before me, my Mamá. Abram became Abraham. Samuel was never the king. Moses was reticent to accept his leadership position and he had much to learn. Muhammad became a leader while remaining a servant, the chroniclers of history say. Prophets are usually amongst the people, believers and unbelievers: teaching, helping and guiding them, or warning and chastising. They don't command to gain comfort or power over their flock. In many ways, prophets grow in front of the people they are called to serve.

I knew all this religious thought came as a result of the harrowing last 24 hours. That mixed with being in my homeland, the Palenque, the gathering place of my ancestors. Somewhere deep inside me I also knew I was going to come out of this experience a different person, the mother of a changed family.

Chapter Sixteen

SEVERAL WEEKS HAVE PASSED SINCE our family adventure in Mexico. We stopped an invasion, and I rediscovered my children, again, finding out they weren't children anymore. Our shipments of raw cacao beans began again, thanks to Horado's trip to help the Council set up the logistics. Paco spent more time with Horado at the warehouse. They figured out how to accomplish the roasting and dehusking there prior to bringing the cacao home to the chocolate room. I taught Adelita how to roast the beans, then put them into the mechanical crusher to break the cocoa beans into bits and remove most of the fat. We put these bits into a grinder to make the chocolate into a pulpy powder. It was a process that could create quite a mess, but I reminded Adelita that our ancestors had to do all this by hand before they had machines. I demonstrated that if the gooey powder is left in the machine too long, it starts to liquefy, and it took twice as long to clean up. On the other hand, if we didn't grind it enough, it wouldn't come out smooth enough for our expected quality.

'We want our chocolate to be of a high enough quality,' I explained to Adelita, "that it doesn't take away from the more important chocolate space we hope to create with those we share our chocolate with. I used to fear that if we made it too good, it would also take away from the chocolates space experience and become the center of attention. I found out that was impossible. The better the chocolate, the more breadth and depth of the chocolate space."

After the raw chocolate reached the perfect consistency, we added our secret spices. We always added Mexican vanilla, but also sometimes cinnamon, or tarragon, or chili powder, or even saffron. We stored the chocolate in our refrigerators and pressed it into chocolate bars with our family swirl symbol.

"We never let the chocolate get too cold, but we didn't want it to get too hot or dry either."

I assigned Adelita to read some of the internet news feeds and other news sources and she of course talked with Tio Ignacio every day. Once a week we planned to send out chocolates to leaders and people in a position to make a difference. Sometimes we had emergencies and we dropped whatever we were doing to get the chocolate delivered. We also made a special chocolate that wasn't hard on the stomachs of suffering children in different parts of the world. They may not be struggling with weighty decisions, but they need an infusion of hope in their chocolate space.

Horado asked Adelita to hand-write a short note to each person we send chocolate to, explaining it was to help them with their patience, their feelings, and communication between their stomach, their heart and their minds. Sometimes we would get indirect feedback, but mostly we were kept wondering if our chocolate made a difference in each specific instance.

Paco, because it was his idea to start a Chocolate4Peace website, built it with the help of his science teacher at school. He asked to manage the site and is on his way to becoming quite an impressive website developer. We try our best to keep track of problems around the world, but Horado and I reminded Paco and Adelita not to make any judgment about who was right and who was wrong. We continue to send chocolate to people all over the world and put that information on our website so other people, mostly young people can send notes. The website has become a huge hit. A surprise added benefit of the website has been that those who received the chocolate are able to see from the website that we had sent it so they could make sure it was safe to eat and that it had a purpose beyond eating good chocolate. Only three months after launching the website, several large IT companies quietly made an offer to buy Chocolate4Peace because its membership is more populated than some small countries. We quietly replied with a no thanks message, and we are hopefully doing a good job of keeping our operations secret and not connected to us personally. Adelita has mentioned more than once how fun it is to go to school and hear people talking about Chocolate4Peace and not one even knowing our family was the inventor.

Adelita's teacher, Miss Topkins even got into the excitement of Chocolate4Peace. Not long ago, in class, Miss Topkins provided this cute handout:

Chocolate Math

1. Pick the number of times a week that you would like to eat a piece of chocolate (more than once, but less than ten times).

   _____

2. Multiply this number by 2 (because chocolate is so yummy)

   $\times 2 = $ _____

3. Add 5 (for a Saturday treat)

   $+ 5 = $ _____

4. Multiply it by 50.

   $\times 50 = $ _____

5. If you have already had your birthday this year, add 1770 to the number. If you haven't had your birthday, add 1769 to the number. Miss Topkins said that in years later we would need to add one to 1770 and 1769 for every year after 2020.

= _____

6. Now, subtract the four-digit year that you were born from the number.

- (year born) = _____

7. You should have a three-digit number.

_____

Here is the part that wowed Adelita. It turns out the first digit is the number of times you said you wanted to eat chocolate per week and the next two numbers are your age! I wanted to tell her it was just a mathematical self-fulfilling prophecy, but that would take the fun out of it.

Horado started painting more seriously. His portrait of my Mamá was good. Not great, but good. After we all lauded his final product, he shared a surprise with me. "

He took me to our library and stared at the painting of Tio Ignacio for a moment and then turned to me saying, "I visited the museum when I was in Mexico, before I left to meet up with you and Paco."

"You visited a museum?" I asked. "Like with paintings, or ancient artifacts and history?"

"Sort of both," he explained. "I didn't want to bring it up with Paco there. It's kind of a secret."

"A secret museum?" I asked. I was getting tired of asking questions. "Sorry, just tell me about it. I will listen."

"It is a Pochteca museum," Horado began. "It's where Tio Ignacio was at before he came to the family. It is where the portrait that was done of your Mamá will be stored."

"Wait," I said. "I know, I promised no questions, but what is a Pochteca museum? The Pochteca were Aztec merchants in the ancient world, right?"

"The Pochteca were long-distance traders, yes," Horado said. "They were mostly Aztec, but over the decades and centuries of trade between the Mayans and the Aztecs, there was a Pochteca guild among the Mayans also. They were cacao traders. The Aztecs wanted all they could get. The Mayans controlled that trade. In addition to trade, they were warriors. They had to be because of all the places outside of the Aztec and Mayan empires that they traveled. The Aztecs often employed them as spies to keep tabs on their enemies, and their friends. The Mayan Pochteca guild became skilled artisans as well as traders. They learned artistic skills in carving, weaving, pottery, and painting from artisans from as far away as what we now call North America and as far south as the altiplano of the Andes mountains. There may have even been contact with other parts of the world. There is a lacquerware of the Purépecha from the area that is now Michoacán in Mexico that is only found elsewhere in China. There are stories of Middle Eastern contact also, as you know. I saw paintings at the Pochteca Guild Museum that looked like they were out of a Byzantine Court."

"Have you ever been to a Byzantine court Horado?" I asked. "Sorry, no questions. Go on."

"Somewhere these long-distance travelers picked up talents and abilities that together created something otherworldly," Horado said in hushed tones. "I didn't just show up and visit this place. I was invited. Not by a person, or even a talking painting. It was a feeling. And when I showed up the old man at the door smiled at me and let me in without a word. It is a small place and I mentioned that to the caretaker. He looked at me and said, "The Pochteca became very adept at hiding their wealth. They were wealthy traders but did not want to cause the ire of the aristocratic class. That translated into their ability to hide some of their most important discoveries."

Horado looked at Tio Ignacio and then back to me. "That is how I found out it was a Pochteca museum. The man, who never told me his name, knew your name, and said I was welcome to bring you to see the museum. I want to do that soon if we can."

"I want to go, Horado," I said with emotion that surprised me. "I want to be a part of every facet of your life. You know I love museums."

"Querida, I think I am supposed to be one of the Pochteca painters," Horado said with a little awe in his voice and fear in his eyes.

"Do you want to?" I asked.

"Yes," Horado said. "I think I do. I doubt my talent, I doubt my wisdom, but I have to admit I love holding a brush with paint on it. The one thing I know is, I can't do it, though, without you. That is not my desire or my doubt speaking. I think this is a two-person endeavor. My passion and your wisdom."

Señor Nietzsche said something like, "myth can only be understood as a symbolic picture of Dionysian wisdom by means of Apollonian art," I said.

"What?" Horado asked. "You completely lost me."

"Something from my university days," I explained. "I have K'abel Xiu to thank for remembering that quote. Remember the test I had to retake? It was on Greek and Roman mythology. Some things are etched in my memory forever."

"That's why you remember it," Horado said with arched eyebrows, "but what in the Mole Poblano does it mean?"

"There is this tension in Greek art and word, between Apollo and Dionysus perspectives," I began. "Apollo and Dionysus are both sons of Zeus, the Greek head god. Apollo is the god of the sun and of rational thinking and order. He represents logic, prudence and purity. Dionysus is the god of wine and dance and represents irrationality and chaos, emotions and instincts. Some say, art cannot be understood without the tension between the two."

"So, I'm the Dionysus and you are the Apollo?" Horado asked. "That makes sense."

"Or it's the other way around, Horado," I suggested. "It is also our family business. Helping people make the decision from their heart to the mind and back.

"I never saw it like that," Horado said. "I mean, I never thought of Apollo and Dionysus at all, but I never considered you and me as the metaphor for the family business. Together we make the round trip."

"To live with you, Horado, is to find joy in the good times and in the hard times," I said kissing his cheek. "Just like plants grow from the rain of a fearsome storm, peace, understanding, and happiness come from finding meaning in hard things. You bring meaning into my life. When we know who we are and that we have a purpose and can make a difference, we can face the hard or scary times and be just like our children, Paco and Adelita."

"Our warrior children," Horado said with a prideful smile.

"Maybe, but I have come to think of them as servant-leaders, more humble, meek, and peace-seeking."

"In a world of celebrity, selfishness, and winning means someone else has to lose, how did we raise these two children?" Horado asked.

"The ego-centric warrior lives a life of glory mostly battling the fear of obscurity," I said. "The servant-leader would rather remain anonymous and ensure the success of the mission and the soldiers that make it happen." I got up from my favorite chair in my favorite room with my favorite person. "Let's go find our peaceable-walking-warriors and give them a hug."

My Mamá visited later that night. She surprised us all in giving Paco his third name. The name she gave him was Janaab.

It means flower, well specifically the water lily. Adelita was shocked and said so. She thought Mamá was joking.

"That sounds like a girl name," Adelita said. "He is a guy, a tough guy." Then she stopped speaking and seemed to be listening. She nodded and smiled. Then she said, "Tio Ignacio says that in Mayan culture, the flower is connected with creation and hope. Some ancient Mayan warriors were experts at plundering—just taking things in a mean way, but the greatest were builders and creators. Those warriors proudly wore the symbol of the water lily."

"Ah, this is true," my Mamá said. She turned to her grandchildren and continued. "The Mayans had jaguar protectors. They considered these protectors to be ancestors. These protectors were painted on shields and is one of the most painted forms in their art and stone carvings. One of the most powerful and important was the Water Lily Jaguar, called that because he had a water lily on his head. He can also transform, often into fire."

"My brother is a transformer," Adelita said. "Cool."

Paco remained silent.

His Abuela continued. "Our ancestors are from Palenque. One of its most famous rulers was K'inich Pakal, That is where your first name comes from, and your second. His name was also Janaab. It seemed fitting that your third name should come from him. He ruled for sixty-eight years. That is the longest reign in the millennium in which he lived, the second longest in the history of the Americas, and the fifth longest in the entire world. With this name comes a long life, the power to be as fierce as fire when you must, but always be the protector."

"Gracias, Abuela," Paco said. "From Paco to protector, to fire spectre. I will be a respecter of this life vector."

"Mamá," Adelita said looking at me. "I have something to share with you and Abuela, from Tio Ignacio, if that is alright." Adelita was quiet for a moment and then said, "First, Tio Ignacio congratulates you Paco on your very fitting third name." Another pause from Adelita. "He says it is his honor to serve the quiet, unsung warriors of this family. He says, "The world bows not to the brutal conqueror, but to the meek mother. This humble warrior faces death while creating life. She is strong because she knows what it's like to be weak. She is mighty not because she bravely wields a sword, but because she pressed on into the dark despite her fear." I'm not sure I understand all of that, but Tio Ignacio says you and Abuela will understand."

Adelita showed surprise as her Abuela and I looked at her with tears in our eyes. "There will be a day sometime in the future when I will remind you of those words my mighty warrior," I said to Adelita.

* * *

By the end of the school year, Paco and Adelita were fully involved in our family business and I couldn't imagine how we could do it without them. The family Chocolate4Peace project had added a new dimension to our mission, and we had become significantly more efficient in getting chocolate to the right people at the right time.

"Just think Mamá," Adelita commented to me, "what if more children around the world could send chocolate bars to world leaders and people who needed a lift." I explained that our principal goal was to help create chocolate space, but as we mailed boxes of chocolate to the Mayor of Mexico City and the Mexican President, I wondered if her thought was more profound than I had first considered.

"This has been a crazy year so far Mamá," she continued. "First the Chocolate Room and then finding out you are a chemistry and chocolate expert, then hearing Tio Ignacio, discovering Paco is a super smart and brave brother who still has stinky shoes, traveling to Mexico to stop an invasion, becoming friends with

Lady Xiu and her family, and now we are working together to become smarter about the world and who needs our help. You were right, we really are making a difference! Next thing you will tell me is, Papá is a superhero," she said with a laugh.

"Who do you think held up the street while I was doing the construction of the Chocolate Room?" I asked with a knowing smile.

Epilogue

To close the loop on how things ended up with K'abel Xiu and our family, she escorted Adelita and my Mamá home, arriving the day after Horado, Paco, and me. We listened to their stories and K'abel complimented Adelita on her wisdom and on her bravery. Adelita somehow remained humble after all she had accomplished and was embarrassed but thanked K'abel for the best weekend of her life. I was secretly grateful that I had been a witness, thanks to Paco's insistence we back up Adelita, and Horado's masterful preparation and execution. Adelita replied that Lady Xiu was a Mayan Queen and had acted like it in front of a bunch of "mean and scary people." K'abel was embarrassed too. She hugged Adelita and gave me a kind smile before leaving. I wondered if our paths would ever cross again.

After K'abel Xiu left, the first thing Adelita said was, "It was you guys, right?"

"I'm not sure what you are talking about," I replied, "But I am grateful your Papá has kept up his talent for poison dart shooting with a blowgun."

Adelita smiled. No more was said.

Adelita slept for an entire day and didn't really get back to normal for a week. K'abel Xiu took a day off I assume, but when she was dropping off Adelita, she seemed to be ten years younger in age and energy.

The next Monday at school Adelita saw Bembe. He was assigned to the other sixth grade class. Adelita told me she was fine with that. "I have a feeling we are going to see a lot of each other in the coming days and years," she shared with a smile.

K'abel Xiu came by our home a few days later by herself. Horado was at the warehouse and Paco and Adelita were in school. "Do you have a moment, Chimalmat?" K'abel asked.

I sucked in a breath. That was the first time I had been called by that name, my name, in years. It sounded almost foreign.

"I'm sorry," I heard K'abel say, as I refocused on her face. I noticed she had tears collecting in her eyes. "I didn't mean to cause such a shock, but I deserve it. I have been terrible to you and to your family for many years. I wanted to ask your forgiveness. I will do so in writing, so you don't have to see me." She turned to leave. And just as quickly turned back and added, "You daughter is just like you. I was in awe of you, and it came out as extreme jealousy when we were younger. I don't want that to happen again. I assume she told you what happened. Far more than the events that took place, it was my honor that you entrusted her in my care." She turned again and walked to her car.

I had not recovered from hearing my name when she shared these other words with me. I felt like I had been mortared up in a brick wall and was unable to make the air in my lungs create sounds. I could only do one thing. I ran to her, grabbed her shoulders, and turned her to me. I think she thought I was going to hit her, or push her, because she flinched, but she didn't try to defend herself. I put my arms around her and began to cry softly. Then K'abel began to cry. Then I began to sob more vocally. That somehow allowed my voice box to function again.

"Come into the house," I said to K'abel. "Two ladies crying in the front yard will cause the neighbors to jump to all kinds of conclusions."

We were silent until we closed the front door behind us. I wiped my face with my hands, smiled and said, "Thank you for making me a noun."

"What?" K'abel asked. "Did I say something wrong? I mean, I know I have said a lot of things wrong over the years, but just now, did I say something wrong?"

"I have a lot of names," I began. "Mamá, hija." I didn't mention 'querida,' dear, that Horado uses, because I didn't know if that would cause an emotional reaction in K'abel. "Being a mother, or a daughter are adjectives. Sometimes those titles feel like nicknames, or like a call sign if I were a pilot. Acknowledging myself as a mother, makes me a verb, an action word. By the end of the day, I often feel 'actioned' completely up." I paused to see if she understood what I was saying. I had my doubts because I really didn't know what I was saying. I just knew it felt right to say it out loud to someone.

K'abel had a concerned look on her face. "Umm, I just wanted to say I'm sorry. I'm not sure where this is going. Maybe I just don't understand what you are trying to say."

"Ay, sorry," I said, trying to put my thoughts on a shelf for another time but unable to do so. I took a breath and tried again. "So much has happened in the past weeks that my emotions are overflowing. It's just that I haven't heard my real first name spoken by someone else in ages. It feels like I am finally a noun again, my core essence. I know, I'm crazy."

"Ha, ha," K'abel laughed. "You are talking to the person who has been chasing an adjective for more than half of my life." She raised her chin in the air, and with a snobby voice said, "You can call me *Lady* Xiu. I very much dislike names. Nouns and verbs as you say. I made some mistakes, as you know. You had a front row seat. Sorry. In that charge to the bottom of my character, I was given a name. A shame name that I must now live with for the rest of my life."

"I have been thinking about that," I admitted. "Not in a bad way at all. In fact, I can't think of anyone else outside of our family I would trust more with my children than you. I had a great, many greats, aunt named Izel. You know the language better than me, but I am pretty sure that means 'unique, the only one.' I have been thinking in my mind of you as Lady Izel."

"I don't think our culture allows for a fourth name, or a "do-over" name," K'abel said.

"We are not the slaves of our culture," I said, determined. "We were not made for our culture, our culture was made by and for us. If I want to change your name, who can stop me?"

"Everyone in my village back home," K'abel said.

"Then I will go to your village and announce the change. If there is anyone who would have the right to do so it is me. It is because of me that you were given your name." I didn't want to mention her third name, *Tuus*, meaning to tell a lie, to cheat, or deceive.

"You have no blame in my actions," K'abel said. "The arrow can't blame the target for striking."

"We'll see," I said. "Anyway, it is a joy to have you in our home. You are forgiven and that part of our past forgotten. Ever since I first saw you, I felt we were destined to be friends. Maybe now that can happen."

"Ever since I first saw you, I felt I was destined to stand in your shadow and it made me mad," K'abel said. "Only now do I realize it was never a shadow that you created, but the warmth that I could have warmed my hands by all these years. So many years, lost."

"No lost years," I corrected. "You have a wonderful family and have done great things."

"Let's please start again," K'abel said. "Hi, my name is K'abel Xiu." She presented her hand.

"Hi, I'm Chimalmat. My friends call me Chima," I said. "I have it from a very reliable source, my Tio Ignacio, that you are a descendent of Lady Ix Tz'akbu Ajaw, the red Queen," I added.

"As you have thought of the name Izel, I have often pondered your name. I do know that Chimalmat means 'mother of giants.' It took Hector and me many years to get pregnant with Bembe. That was another log that fueled my fire against you. It seemed you were guaranteed children and that they would be amazing."

"I always felt my name was a blessing and curse. I have only recently realized I was the one making it a curse. I did have Paco without any problems. Adelita was a particularly challenging pregnancy, however. From day one as a mother, no before I even got married, I have worried whether I could ever live up to my name. It was up to me to be the mother of giants. Anything less would mark failure. Failure to my family and especially to my children. I have seen that I can make a difference, but they will make their own choices. They will make themselves giants. I can't do that for them or force them to it."

"In that case, I have something for you," K'abel said. "I don't always carry this around with me, but I wanted something meaningful to say to you if we were able to talk. I read this years ago and thought of you, the antithesis of me." She pulled out a piece of paper from her purse and handed it to me.

I read it out loud. "Humility is the mother of giants. One sees great things from the valley; only small things from the peak. by G.K. Chesterton, in his book The Innocence of Father Brown." I looked up at K'abel. "Thank you," I said.

"Your humility is your superpower." K'abel began.

I smiled and said, "I told Horado my superpower was Salsa dancing."

"Ha!, just as important as humility, no?" K'abel said laughing. "I have been one of those little things you can see from your peak, but you have always treated me like a great thing."

"Like I said, I have always known, or hoped, we were destined to be friends." I went to the cupboard and pulled out a couple small chocolate bars. I handed one to K'abel. "I have never heard of that author, Chesterton. Are you a reader?"

"I read a lot, but I didn't know the author either until I saw that quote in a magazine. I had to go look him up. I did read the story referenced. Father Brown was a fictional character, a catholic priest who solves mysteries and crimes kind of like Sherlock Holmes."

We talked about books, family, Mexico, and laughed through the afternoon. I thought of yet another purpose of the zygomaticus major muscle. It contributes to laughing, which is why this muscle is sometimes referred to as one of the "laughing muscles". I was surprised when Adelita walked in the door from school. She saw K'abel sitting at our kitchen table. She wasn't surprised at all. She approached K'abel and gave her a hug, smiled, and said, "I'm going to get my homework done now so I can get on the Chocolate4Peace website before dinner." She left without another word.

I listened and heard a door open. It was K'abel's turn to take in a breath and forget to exhale.

Unlike some tribes and organized groups of indigenous peoples of the Americas the Maya never vanished or were completely assimilated. The Mayan civilization has weathered two millennia with cities disappearing or being abandoned, while others were founded and grew. They accomplished wonders in art, science, architecture and agriculture, and will yet accomplish wonders that will bless the contemporary world.

Additional works on sale by this author:
(recent works available at Amazon.com)

Transitions from Military Rule in South America: The Obligational Legitimacy Hypothesis
Published by Naval Postgraduate School Press, 1987, 210 pages
Approved for public release.

Long-term Success: A New Paradigm for Personal and Enterprise Achievement
Published by Byblos Press, June 2003; 40 pages
ISBN 0-9746003-1-8

The Seeds He Planted
Published by Byblos Press, December 2007; 146 pages
ISBN 978-0-9746003-2-1

Nahum's Story
Published by Byblos Press, December 2007; 46 pages
ISBN 978-0-9746003-3-8

Media in the 21st Century: Meet-Up or Meltdown in the Meaning Marketplace
Published by Byblos Media, June 2010; 583 pages
ISBN 978-0-9746003-6-9

Conversations Among Butterflies
Published by Byblos Media, August 2015; 393 pages
ISBN 978-0-9746003-7-6

Kitab Kabbani
Published by Byblos Media, November 2015; 407 pages
ISBN 978-0-9746003-8-3

Chinese Circus
Published by Byblos Media, 2016, 437 pages
ISBN13 978-0-9746003-9-0

Cambalache
Published by Byblos Media, 2017, 451 pages
ISBN13 978-0-9990111-0-2

Finders Weepers, Losers Keepers
Published by Byblos Media, 2017, 195 pages
ISBN13 978-0-999011126

A Caboodle of Blossoms
Published by Byblos Media, 2020, 200 pages
ISBN13 978-0-9990111-4-0

Breakthrough Understanding: A Prompt Journal
Published by Byblos Media, 2022, 205 pages
ISBN13 978-0-9990111-5-7

Chocolate4Peace
Published by Byblos Media, 2022, 184 pages
ISBN13 978-0-9990111-6-4

*For more information and upcoming publications,
see www.story-alchemist.com*

www.ingramcontent.com/pod-product-compliance
Lightning Source LLC
Chambersburg PA
CBHW060218180626
46813CB00007B/2864